P9-BYF-165

CRIME TRAVELERS

BOOK 1

BRAINWASHED

An International Adventure Novel

Featuring Lucas Benes and the NEW RESISTANCE

PAUL AERTKER

FLYING SOLO PRESS

PARIS | BARCELONA | ROME | SEATTLE | LONDON | NEW YORK |

DENVER | HONG KONG | CAPE TOWN | LOS ANGELES | SAN JOSE

For Katherine, Mary, and Andrew

Crime Travelers—Book One: Brainwashed © 2014 by Paul Aertker All rights reserved. This is a work of fiction. Names, characters, places, and incidents either are the product of the author's imagination or are used fictitiously. Any resemblance to actual persons, living or dead, events, or locales is entirely coincidental. No reproduction without prior permission. Discounts available at www.crimetravelers.com.

Library Meta Data
Aertker, Paul
Crime Travelers / Paul Aertker.—2nd ed.
p. 288 cm. 12.7 x 20.32 (5x8 in) — (Brainwashed ; bk. 1)

Summary: While sleeping on the roof of his father's hotel, thirteen-year-old Lucas Benes finds a baby alone and learns that the Good Company has restarted its kidnapping business. Brainwashed (Crime Travelers #1) tracks the secret urban adventures of the New Resistance, a network of international teenage spies. Headquartered in Las Vegas's posh new Globe Hotel, the New Resistance sends its Tier One kids to Paris on its biggest mission to date. Lucas leads a group of friends through the hotspots of Paris—from the catacombs to the Eiffel tower—in an all-out effort to sabotage a brainwashing ceremony that could potentially turn them all into "Good" kids.

Publishers Review: "Reluctant readers rejoice! Ripped from the headlines of the world's leading news outlets, this realistic middle-grade novel weaves actual life events into action-packed fiction for ages eight plus. Readers are transported to Paris without ever leaving the sofa. With one-hundred thirty-six geographic references, this story serves as both fiction novel and travel guide. Crime Travelers: Brainwashed stands as a travel-adventure book that kids and adults will devour. Multicultural, multilingual, international travel, teen action-adventure: this book has it all." © 2014, FSP

Travel—Fiction. 2. Language and languages—Fiction. 3. Conspiracies—Fiction. 4. Kidnapping—Fiction. 5. Brainwashing—Fiction. 6. Geography—Fiction. 7. Multicultural—Fiction. 8. Europe—Fiction. 9. Paris, France—Fiction. Title. Pro 2014
Edited by Brian Luster using The Chicago Manual of Style, 16th edition
Cover Design by Pintado | Maps by Paul Devine | Interior Design by Amy McKnight | © 2014 Paul Aertker and Flying Solo Press, LLC
Printed worldwide

ISBN-13: 978-1-940137-11-7 / eISBN: 978-1-940137-12-4
Library of Congress Control Number: 2013955080
US Copyright Registration Number: TX 7-981-676

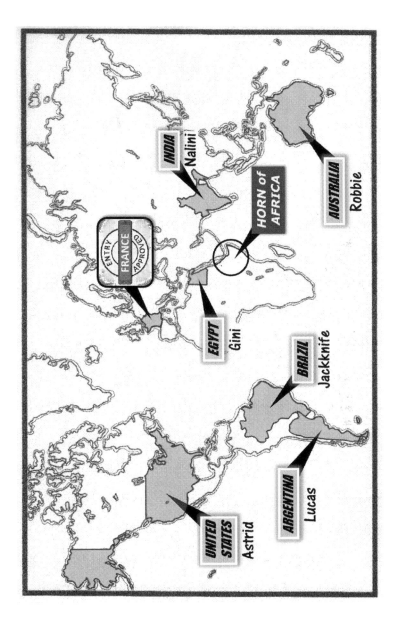

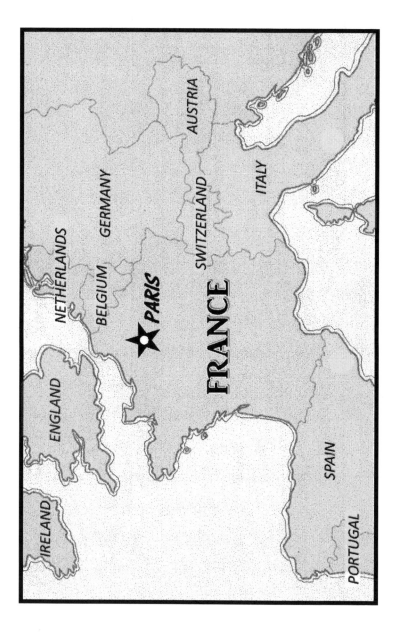

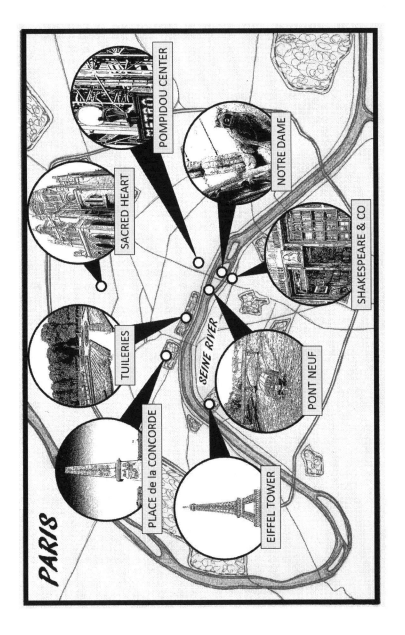

NEW RESISTANCE NOTEBOOK

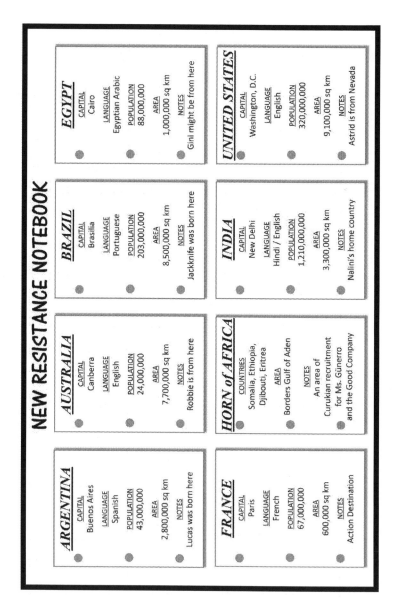

ARGENTINA
- **CAPITAL**
  Buenos Aires
- **LANGUAGE**
  Spanish
- **POPULATION**
  43,000,000
- **AREA**
  2,800,000 sq km
- **NOTES**
  Lucas was born here

AUSTRALIA
- **CAPITAL**
  Canberra
- **LANGUAGE**
  English
- **POPULATION**
  24,000,000
- **AREA**
  7,700,000 sq km
- **NOTES**
  Robbie is from here

BRAZIL
- **CAPITAL**
  Brasilia
- **LANGUAGE**
  Portuguese
- **POPULATION**
  203,000,000
- **AREA**
  8,500,000 sq km
- **NOTES**
  Jackknife was born here

EGYPT
- **CAPITAL**
  Cairo
- **LANGUAGE**
  Egyptian Arabic
- **POPULATION**
  88,000,000
- **AREA**
  1,000,000 sq km
- **NOTES**
  Gini might be from here

FRANCE
- **CAPITAL**
  Paris
- **LANGUAGE**
  French
- **POPULATION**
  67,000,000
- **AREA**
  600,000 sq km
- **NOTES**
  Action Destination

HORN of AFRICA
- **COUNTRIES**
  Somalia, Ethiopia, Djibouti, Eritrea
- **AREA**
  Borders Gulf of Aden
- **NOTES**
  An area of Curukian recruitment for Ms. Gunerro and the Good Company

INDIA
- **CAPITAL**
  New Delhi
- **LANGUAGE**
  Hindi / English
- **POPULATION**
  1,210,000,000
- **AREA**
  3,300,000 sq km
- **NOTES**
  Nalini's home country

UNITED STATES
- **CAPITAL**
  Washington, D.C.
- **LANGUAGE**
  English
- **POPULATION**
  320,000,000
- **AREA**
  9,100,000 sq km
- **NOTES**
  Astrid is from Nevada

CONTENTS

1   The Hotel, the Boat, and the Secret.................. 1

2   A Call to Legs 9

3   You Can't Always Follow the Rules 19

4   Elevator Down 25

5   Baby 32

6   Bat Cave 40

7   The Flying Office 42

8   Child Kidnapping 49

9   The In-Flight Movie 57

10   Curukians 72

11   Who's Watching Whom? 85

12   The Point of No Return 96

13   Master Key, Master Plan 102

14   Room Service 112

15   The Lucky Office 121

16   Curukian Proposal 135

17   Duck in the Duct 144

18   Green Is Good 147

19   A City Crawling with Curukians 153

20   Stink 156

21   The Tour de Paris... 161

22 The Last Best Hiding Place 169

23 The Empire of Death 172

24 Hostile Hostel 179

25 A Meeting of the Minds 183

26 The Truth Behind the Lie 189

27 The Database 193

28 Riding on the Metro 197

29 Pompidou 201

30 A Never-Ending Supply of Curukians 205

31 Carnival of the Animals 208

32 Notre Dame Is Our Lady? 212

33 The Brainwashing Ceremony 218

34 Shakespeare in Paris 229

35 The River Seine 245

36 Carnival 251

37 A New Way to Kidnap 257

38 Busball 268

39 Good Things Happen to Bad People 285

40 A Hotel Is a Home 287

No matter how bad your past is,

you still don't want it erased.

THE HOTEL, THE BOAT, AND THE SECRET

Lucas Benes lay in a sleeping bag on the roof of his father's hotel, dreaming about a past he couldn't remember.

On this particular morning a strange sound woke him and pulled him from the dark. With his eyes still closed, Lucas stayed quiet and tried to take it all in. He could hear the distant hum of tires on the freeways around the city. From somewhere close by a car engine cranked several times and then conked out.

Lucas strained his ears and unzipped the sleeping bag.

Slowly he rolled over, got on one knee, and peered over the rooftop. With his bare chest leaning against the concrete wall he stared down thirteen floors. Lucas watched as the lights in the back parking lot flickered then dimmed. His eyes traveled across the empty, unfilled spaces to the center of the blacktop. There, parked like a regular car between the white lines, was a shopping cart with a baby lying in it, alone.

"What —" he muttered.

Lucas knew what it felt like to be abandoned. When he was two, his mother died just hours after she had adopted him. If he could help it, he wouldn't let another kid be left alone.

Besides, a baby by itself was creepy. And the sooner he got to the kid the better. The stairs would take too long, and everyone in the hotel would slow him down.

Rappelling would be the quickest way. Without wasting a second more he pulled a pair of jeans over his boxers, rolled up his sleeping bag and foam mattress, and stowed them in a camping bin.

He heard the odd noise again.

Behind his basketball hoops and partially hidden in the shadow of a construction dumpster was a dark-colored van. The motor sputtered and struggled to start, a thin cloud of exhaust puffing from its tailpipe. Lucas squinted and tried to commit the license plate to memory. The numbers were dirty, but he was sure he recognized Canadian tags.

Lucas had clocked the last eleven of his thirteen years living in the Globe Hotel, and this parking lot was his backyard. During that time he had seen plenty of older kids join the New Resistance safe houses that were hidden in some of his father's hotels. But he had never witnessed an actual drop-off of another kid.

No one had.

All of a sudden a sliding door slammed shut. With a blast of black smoke the van coughed to a rumble and started moving. It peeled out through piles of construction sand and spun into the parking lot. A single working headlight bumped in the early-morning darkness and appeared to head straight for the baby. The van swerved around the shopping cart, crashed through a wooden barricade, and fishtailed down the street.

In the distance the famous lights of Las Vegas were still shining, with the miniature Eiffel Tower capping the weirdness of his whole life.

Lucas zeroed in on the baby.

If he was fast enough, he could grab the kid and maybe not get in trouble for breaking the "no climbing alone" rule. Nobody broke Coach's rules.

Coach Creed was a giant East Texan with a big hat and boots and a voice to match.

But at that moment, a baby alone in a shopping cart was more important to Lucas than some made-up rule.

Besides, Coach Creed would most likely show up for morning climbing practice in a few minutes and find something Lucas had done wrong anyway.

When he was too quick, Coach would say, "Lucas! You've got to think before you act." The next time Lucas would take too long to think before he acted, Coach would bark, "Lucas, get your head out of the clouds."

The smell of bacon rose from a nearby kitchen vent, and Lucas knew everyone in the hotel would soon be awake. He hurried toward the climbing section and popped open a plastic bin, slipped on a T-shirt and climbing shoes, and strapped on his waist harness. Then he stepped onto a metal platform and grabbed the ropes.

He would rappel down, get the baby, and winch himself and the child up to the roof, hopefully before Coach Creed arrived. He clipped a hook from the winch motor to a carabiner on his harness and unlocked a ratchet.

At the side of the hotel, the morning garbage trucks rolled in and clanged the dumpsters on the concrete pads. The trucks' backup beepers always made Lucas think about his mother dying.

"Focus, Lucas," he mumbled to himself. "Don't think about that accident."

Thirteen floors to the ground.

Lucas had to concentrate. He stepped backward over the ledge, fixed his feet to the outside wall, and settled into the harness.

It was his first solo rappel. His mouth dried to the point where he could taste a new filling in his back molar. Lucas calculated the distance to the parking lot.

Fifty-two meters. One-hundred seventy feet.

He flexed his biceps, wrapped his fingers around the rope, and set the line in the harness to free-fall.

In climbing, there was always a fraction of a second between the security of being locked in and the freedom of an actual rappel.

His heart skipped as he rappelled down the outside wall. The rope began to hum. At the seventh floor he passed the window of his assigned hotel room. When he landed on the ground, he stepped out of the harness and hooked it to the winch that would hoist him back up.

Lucas crept around the building to the back parking lot. And there it was, just like he had seen from the roof—a baby lying in a shopping cart. Lucas's mind went negative.

What if the kid was not alive? He tried to think if he had ever seen a dead person before. He'd never been to a funeral, and he knew he had never seen a dead baby, and he definitely didn't want to.

His heart pounded in his chest.

Lucas walked, tiptoed, toward the shopping cart. The last of the parking lot lights flickered out, leaving only the early morning sun. He moved across the blacktop, making sure not to step on a white line. At this moment he needed all the luck he could get. As he got closer to the cart, he held his breath and swallowed.

He gripped the shopping cart handle and looked over into the basket. He gasped.

The van he had seen only moments earlier came flying back into the parking lot. The tires screeched across the asphalt, burning a cloud of white smoke. Lucas's eyes doubled in size as he watched the van's single headlight come barreling directly at him.

The baby, he thought.

Lucas unglued his knuckles from the shopping cart handlebars and pushed. He watched as the wheels wobbled, rolling the cart just out of the way. He turned back to see the van. Three seconds, he calculated, and he would be dead.

Lucas could see the driver's face. A teenager.

At the last second the boy jammed the brakes and cut the wheel.

The two-ton vehicle dipped in the front and then spun one hundred eighty degrees so that the back doors faced Lucas.

He couldn't believe his luck—but in Las Vegas luck was not always good.

The rear doors crashed open and two dark figures, maybe boys, grabbed Lucas and pulled him into the van.

Lucas hit his head on the metal wall and dropped to the floor.

There he rolled into a pile of balls—basketballs and footballs. He settled on what felt like a clump of golf balls jamming him in the back.

The two boys were wearing black shirts and pants, and they both seemed to have thin fuzzy mustaches.

One boy got behind Lucas and put him in a full nelson while the other stretched a piece of duct tape across Lucas's mouth.

The boy gripped the roll of tape in his fist and leaned over Lucas. "Don't say a word," he whispered.

Duh, Lucas thought. *I've got duct tape on my mouth.*

"You stupid," said the other boy. "He can't talk."

The second boy then let Lucas out of the full nelson and ripped the tape from his face.

"Ah!" Lucas yelped as his cheeks burned. "Who are you?"

"Don't worry about who we are," said the second boy.

Lucas licked his lips, working the tape glue from his skin.

"What's going on?" asked Lucas. "You trying to kidnap me? And why did you drop that baby off like that?"

The two boys looked at each other.

"I told you he had seen us," said the first boy.

"Listen," said the second boy. "We're not kidnapping you."

The other boy added, "We just want to make sure you don't tell anyone."

"Tell anyone what?" asked Lucas. "About the baby?"

"No," said the first boy. "We left a note about the baby. It'll tell you everything you need to know."

"You can read it when we're gone," said the other. "It's just that no one can know we are here now."

"Why?" asked Lucas.

"We're working in secret," said both boys.

The first boy added, "If you tell anyone you saw us, we'll never be able to help again."

"But why?" asked Lucas.

"Why?" repeated the boy. "Why? Because she'll kill us."

"Or worse," said the second boy, "brainwash us like the others."

Lucas was confused. "Who are you talking about?"

The two boys laughed.

"Siba Günerro," said the first boy, shaking his head.

"Head of the Good Company."

Lucas closed his eyes.

He wanted to forget about what had happened the last time he had a run-in with Ms. Günerro. The Good Company was, after all, the suspected world leader in kidnapping children.

Everyone at the New Resistance believed Siba Günerro and her Good Company were responsible for blowing up the ferryboat that had killed his adoptive mother some eleven years earlier.

Lucas sat up. "If you didn't want me to see you, then why did you come back into the parking lot?"

"I spotted you spying on us from the roof," said the first boy. "We had to make sure."

The other boy asked, "What were you doing on the roof anyway?"

Lucas was getting tired of this game. "I live in a hotel and go to hotel-school with the same people that I've been with since I was two," he said. "The roof is the only place to get away around here."

The driver yelled into the back of the van. "He's lying."

Immediately the van clunked into gear and lurched forward.

The balls rolled around as Lucas and the two boys flipped over and fell into each other.

Kidnapping was Lucas's second greatest fear.

A CALL TO LEGS

As the van drove through the parking lot, it skidded sideways.

A cardboard box tipped over and hundreds of new balls flooded the back of the van. Lucas slapped a basketball out of his way as he turned his attention to his escape.

The van's tires bumped over the broken barricade. They were leaving the parking lot. He really was being kidnapped. Or detained. Either way he didn't like it. The van sped up again and all three boys lost their balance and slid down the floor and into the balls bobbing around the back doors.

One of the boys panicked and yelled to the driver, "Stop!"

The van came to an abrupt and jarring halt. For Lucas, it was an opportunity.

He rolled over and jammed his feet into the doors, kicking them as hard as he could.

The back doors flew open. The driver hit the gas, and Lucas, the two boys, and hundreds of balls crashed into the parking lot.

Lucas glared at the two boys. He noticed one of the

boys had a huge scar on his neck.

"If you're not trying to kidnap me," Lucas said, "then why did you just try to drive off with me still in the van?"

"That's our driver," said the boy with the scar. "He's worried we won't make our flight to Paris."

"We're on your side," the other boy said. "You've got to believe us."

"You can't tell anyone you saw us," said the boy with the scar. "Promise?"

Maybe it was something in their voices, the way they were pleading, hoping for a win of some kind— for whatever reason Lucas believed them.

"I promise," he said.

The two boys nodded and took off sprinting after the van that was now speeding away from the hotel.

Lucas hurried toward the shopping cart. He didn't know what he would do with the baby once he got there. He spotted a wadded blanket of some kind under the cart. Lucas squeezed the handle and peered into the shopping basket.

The baby appeared to be breathing. She or he looked like someone's little brother or sister. Lucas still didn't know what to do. He reached for the note.

From the rooftop he heard Coach Creed's voice blasting out. "Lucas!"

"I am in so much trouble," Lucas muttered as he left the baby and the note behind. He raced back to the climbing section, where he quickly slipped on the waist harness and hit the UP button on the winch motor.

"Ugh," he groaned.

Failed again. Climbing solo was an automatic F.

The winch motor began to churn, hoisting Lucas back to the roof. He looked up and saw Astrid, his fourteen-year-old sister, her blond hair draping over the roof's edge like Rapunzel.

Behind her Coach Creed stood with his beefy arms folded.

As soon as Lucas was back on the rooftop, he dropped his head and prepared for yet another lecture. Astrid crossed her arms. She looked so mad that she couldn't even talk.

Coach Creed picked up a bag of climbing chalk. He waited for a second and then tugged on his belt and shook his head.

"Lucas," he said. "You've got to think before you act."

"I did think," said Lucas, defensively. "I thought I should help that baby."

Coach Creed eyed Lucas like an angry principal. "Don't talk back to me."

Astrid and Coach stared at each other, and then slowly turned their heads toward Lucas.

They spoke at the same time. "What baby?"

For a split second Lucas questioned what had actually just happened to him. But he knew what had happened. He didn't have to tell them about the boys in the van, but he did have to tell them about the kid. "There's a baby in a shopping cart in the back parking lot," explained Lucas, taking the bag of chalk from Coach.

"Nobody's allowed back there," said Coach Creed. "That construction zone has a hole as big as Texas going straight down to the new underground dorms they're building."

"You can go and look for yourself," said Lucas. "There's a baby down there. Honest."

"Not possible," said Coach Creed. "And we don't have time for your games. Certainly not today."

"Let me guess," Astrid added. "This is another Lucas dream where you're saving somebody. Oh, it's a baby this time."

"There was a . . ." Lucas started to say. "Forget it." This kind of argument was typical for Lucas.

No one ever believed him. He knew it would be quicker and easier just to follow Coach's rules and master this rappel through the window.

Astrid's eyes were sharp. "You're just trying to get out of doing this window rappel that you can never get right anyway," she sassed. "We'll never find out what happened to my mother or yours if you don't learn what you're supposed to do. . . ."

Lucas's mind drifted back.

The Globe Hotel employees had retold the tragedy so many times that Lucas felt like he partly remembered the accident happening to him.

An explosion on dark water.

Lucas replayed the story in his head one more time:

When Astrid was three, her mother secretly went to Argentina to adopt several children. After she signed the papers, baby Lucas, the other children, and their newly adoptive mother—Astrid's actual birth mother—boarded a ferry. Moments later the boat hit a freak iceberg, sank, and everyone on board was killed.

Except Lucas.

Suddenly two uniformed security guards burst through a stairwell door and onto the roof, snapping Lucas out of his daydream.

The guards were wearing thin jackets with breast patches clearly visible: NEW RESISTANCE SECURITY. The men walked quickly, their shoes crunching the gravel.

The officers were not even halfway across the rooftop when Coach Creed cocked his head toward them and barked, "Now what is it?"

"Cancel the climbing practice," said the first guard. "Already?" Coach Creed asked. "Lucas is not ready for Tier One."

The guard's voice was firm and serious. "Mr. Benes just issued a Call to Legs."

The other guard finished. "He said she's planning another event, a big one, in France this time."

Astrid gathered her blond hair behind her. "Who?" Lucas already knew the answer.

"Who else?" said the first guard. "Siba Günerro."

The dreaded name sank in: Siba Günerro. She and her Good Company could only mean bad news.

Coach Creed turned around to face the security guards. As usual, the top of his Texas-sized butt crack was in full view.

"Lucas said there was a baby in the back parking lot," he said. "Can't imagine it being true. Go check it out anyway."

As the guards left, Coach hiked up his pants and returned his attention to Lucas and Astrid.

"I hate what happened to your mothers," he said. "But the only way you'll ever get over this is to get even."

"I don't want to get even with the Good Company," snapped Lucas.

"My mom died in that accident!" Astrid said. "All you got was a fear of dark water. How could you not want revenge? My mother saved you by sticking you in that ice chest. You could be dead or, worse, part of the Good Company now!"

Lucas slammed the bag of climbing chalk on the roof. "I'm sorry," he said. "I know I should care but—"

Coach broke in. "We have to go. A Call to Legs means we're all getting on an airplane in less than an hour, and we've got to coordinate with New Resistance teams all over the world."

"Never mind," Lucas said with a shrug. At that moment he just wanted to hurry and find out what was going on with the baby. He groaned, "I don't want to go to hotel-school, and I don't want to train for something I'll never use. And I don't want to go to France, either. But what I think never matters anyway. So let's get this over with."

A big grin came over Coach's face. "You mean you don't want me pushing you?" he asked playfully. "Pushing you like this?"

Coach Creed locked his elbow and stiff-armed Lucas in the chest, moving him back to the edge of the climbing platform.

"No, please," said Lucas. "Not again."

"Training is over," said Coach. "I swapped out the glass window on your room with sugar glass, and it's going to be melting as soon as the sun hits it. You and Astrid need to rappel down to that window and get on an elevator and on the plane with everybody else. Understood?"

The problem for Lucas was not what Coach was saying but who was saying it.

Sure, it was Coach's job—that's what teachers do—they push kids to be better. But Lucas wanted his dad to be teaching him something. Only his dad was like a lot of fathers . . . always working and never at home.

"Don't worry. You're from Vegas." Coach grinned at Lucas. "Room 777—triple sevens. Could be lucky."

Lucas gripped the rope at his waist, stretched out

over the edge, and prepared to jump. The full sun came over the roofline, and Lucas turned his head away from the light.

He had to get it right this time.

Things had been off course for Lucas since . . .

It all went back to the day after the ferryboat accident. Nuns from the Good Hospital had found him floating in a Styrofoam ice chest in the sea near Tierra del Fuego.

With him they found a tiny bell and a numbered birth chart. Lucas remembered reading the doctors' notes. They had listed him as an FLK— a Funny Looking Kid with bed head. From that time on everything in Lucas's life seemed to grow unmistakably crooked.

Coach looked over the edge of the roof and blocked the morning sunlight. "Lucas, get your head out of the clouds."

Typical. Lucas had taken too long to act.

Coach shook his massive hand at Lucas. "What are you doing? We've got a Call to Legs in France and you're daydreaming. You're not thinking about that boat wreck again, now are you?"

Lucas shook his head.

He hated it when Coach Creed got mad but he knew the Texan was right.

Coach raised a stopwatch high in the air and

The underground grotto was so big it could have held three hotels inside it. Wall sconces cast spots of light on the stone floors. Above their heads giant ventilation fans spun in the dark, bringing fresh air into the cave. They could hear the music teacher, Mr. Siloti, playing a piano in the music room.

A long series of moving sidewalks cut straight down the middle of this grand hallway.

On the right-hand side there were two janitors—one pushing a wheeled trash can, the other polishing the floor with a machine. On the left, construction workers were building brand-new dorm rooms for the expected arrival of new students. With so many world problems, more and more street kids from all over the planet were starting to show up at Globe Hotels to join the New Resistance.

"Everybody's already gone," Astrid said as she hurried toward the moving sidewalk. "We're going to miss our flight."

She hit a button just below the handrail that read HIGH SPEED.

With Gini in his arms, Lucas followed Astrid and stepped onto the moving sidewalk. The mat picked up speed as they passed the construction zone, the janitors, and the communications center. They broke into a run, past the gym, the film studio, the new student café—aptly named Grotto—finally coming to the end of the sidewalk. There they hopped on a waiting bullet train. In minutes the train transported them underground to the main airplane hangar twenty miles into the Mojave Desert.

The Boeing 747 Intercontinental airliner took up most of the hangar. The multistory jet was the longest passenger aircraft in the world. Manufactured in Seattle and customized with Destination Dispatch and Stealth Technology, the airliner was arguably the world's most modern.

At the New Resistance, this jet was known simply as White Bird One.

Once they were inside the hangar, Lucas, Gini, and Astrid moved even more quickly as the place was buzzing with excited activity. A fire truck with lights flashing followed a fuel truck to the front of the plane. The crew scurried like ants, giving the airplane its final check. Baggage handlers loaded boxes and luggage onto a conveyor belt. Mechanics with clipboards inspected the wings. A small tug truck pulled a cart loaded with engines. And security guards circled the room on mountain bikes. From the back of the airplane a flight attendant whistled at them.

"Hurry up," she yelled, waving her hand excitedly.

The threesome shot across a concrete floor and up the airplane's back staircase. Lucas scanned the section for a seat. The entire plane was first class, with each row having only two giant swivel seats that converted into beds, one on each side of the aisle. Lucas and Gini took a seat near the second-floor staircase. Astrid sat across from them.

The seats were ultramodern oversized pods tricked out with everything anyone might ever need or want. Lucas opened an armrest and found a minifridge packed with food and drinks, snacks and candy. Without a thought he cracked open a tiny Coke.

"Oh yeah! Upgrade," Lucas bragged as if he were the one who had actually made it all happen. He guzzled the Coke and gave Gini a sip. "Can babies drink Coke?"

"I don't think so," said Astrid.

The British voice from the elevator speaker returned.

"Thanks so much for riding with us. Buckle those belts and do have a pleasant day."

Lucas set Gini between his legs and ran a seat belt around both of their waists. He looked over at Astrid and dropped his shoulders.

"Don't worry, Astrid. I'm in," Lucas said calmly. He patted down the baby's thin black hair. "Me and Gini are in."

"Gini and I," said Astrid, correcting his grammar.

Gini puffed out her fat cheeks, looked at Astrid, and farted.

CHAPTER 6

BAT CAVE

Inside the airplane white LED lights on the ceiling faded to a cool blue. The lighting and soft music seemed to have a calming effect on everyone. Gini dozed in Lucas's seat while he rested his forehead on the cool window and watched.

In a remote section of the Mojave Desert north of Las Vegas, the side of a rocky mountain rumbled open like an enormous garage door. A flock of bats flew out into the morning sky as White Bird One emerged from the hangar.

Lucas watched as a line of six street sweepers motored out of the cave and accelerated past the crew. The machines dropped their round metal brushes and powered down the desert floor, turning it into a makeshift airstrip. Within minutes the street sweepers disappeared in a cloud of dust, leaving the airplane alone on the desert-floor runway.

"Mr. Benes," said the captain over the PA system, "this is Captain Bannister. Prepare for takeoff."

Fire hissed from four engines as the all-white jet screeched down the desert runway with more than 290 kilonewtons of thrust. In seconds the airplane shot into a clear blue Nevada sky. The aircraft hit Mach .85, traveling nearly the speed of sound and cruising at more than ten thousand meters above the continent.

Lucas didn't really know what to do with Gini, so he did what he would do for himself. He reclined his seat pod into a bed and let the baby doze next to him. It wasn't long thereafter that Lucas too was fast asleep. He drifted back into a dream about his past.

THE FLYING OFFICE

Etta's voice came over the intercom. "Attention all Tier One students. Meeting in five minutes in the main boardroom."

Lucas woke from his dream, where he'd seen an iceberg and an explosion on water. He shook it off quickly, hoping to be picked for Tier One even though he knew he had broken the "no climbing alone" rule. He suddenly felt burdened by the baby in his lap, and he really did not want to change a diaper. Behind him an automatic door to the back galley slid open with a swoosh.

The newest New Resistance flight attendant, Emerald Cavendish, strolled down the aisle carrying her smartphone. She *looked* like a flight attendant—blue suit, red scarf, and auburn hair in a ponytail. Lucas thought he might have found a solution to his baby problem. He unbuckled his seat belt, picked Gini up, and followed Emerald.

The door to the next compartment was also automatic and slid open as she approached. The boardroom was an oval-shaped room with a large mahogany table in the center. About twenty or so students sat in regular airplane seats that both surrounded the table and lined the walls.

The room looked like a video-game testing ground. Groups of teenagers with their legs over armrests worked on laptops and talked quietly into headsets. Monitors flashed with news and cryptic data in hundreds of languages. At the front of the room a smart board showed a global map with tiny flashing lights. Emerald tidied up, picking up flip-flops and empty bags of chips.

"Tier One at the table," she called out. "Ground crew—window seats. Everyone else, out. Let's go."

There was a commotion as kids changed seats. Once everyone was seated, Lucas realized that every eye was on him.

"What?" Lucas said.

His mood changed, and he now felt a surge of defiance with a toddler in his arms. He faced the boardroom full of people. "It's a baby," he grumbled. "Never seen a baby before? I found it—her, I mean—in the back parking lot. By herself. She was kidnapped by Siba Günerro."

Dressed in a gray sport coat and black shirt, John Benes, CEO of the Globe Hotels and New Resistance president, came down the front stairs and into the boardroom of White Bird One. He pushed his slightly graying, short black hair to the side while his blue eyes darted behind rectangular glasses.

"Un-*be*-lievable," he said, walking toward Lucas.

"Ms. Günerro hasn't tried to kidnap babies since"—he shook his head—"since the ferryboat disaster."

The room fell silent. Everyone knew that Mr. Benes carried a dark scar on his heart for the captain, crew, and eight adopted children who had died at sea. But most of all, for the wife he lost. He smiled faintly at Lucas and tousled his hair.

"And who do we have here?" Mr. Benes said, taking the baby.

"Gini," said Lucas. "There was a note in a shopping cart. It said her name was Gini and she was brought here—to our hotel—from Vancouver."

"Everyone," Mr. Benes said, "I would like to introduce you to Gini."

Mr. Benes looked directly across the room at two fifth-year seniors in high school: Robbie Stafford and Sophia Carson.

"Excellent prediction, Robbie," Mr. Benes said. "This proves it. Gini is obviously the first of many attempted kidnappings. I honestly didn't think the Good Company would actually try babies again, but you were right all along. I'll make a note of it in your scholarship recommendation."

Robbie lit up after hearing the compliment and nodded his head respectfully.

Mr. Benes turned back to Lucas.

"Lucas, I want you to take a Tier One seat at the table."

A Tier Two boy with sandy hair spoke up. "I

thought you had to pass all the tests to be Tier One?" said the boy. "I heard Lucas broke the 'no climbing alone' rule."

"We all heard that, Terry," Mr. Benes said. "Thank you for your concern."

Mr. Benes turned back to Lucas. "First of all, Lucas, you're obviously man enough to know when to break a rule to help somebody in need. And that takes courage. I'm very proud," Mr. Benes said. "Second, you're close enough to completing all the tests. And tomorrow is your birthday. Don't worry, we'll have a party for you when we get back." Mr. Benes looked around the boardroom. "Right now, though, it's time you found out—that we all found out—what the Good Company is really up to."

Lucas gave his father a great big smile.

Mr. Benes moved into a more serious tone. "I'm afraid Ms. Günerro has something particularly sinister up her sleeve this time, and I think Robbie is right on track with the information he and Sophia intercepted yesterday."

He turned to Lucas. "And you're actually the only one with this kind of firsthand experience. So you're a perfect person for this Tier One job."

Astrid came in and sat at the table. "Yeah, but he was only a baby then."

Mr. Benes nodded. "Our minds never really forget anything. Memories are always there, somewhere. You just have to tap into them. Your memory is the purest form of time travel."

Coach Creed came down the stairs, talking on his cell phone in Wolof. Coach ended his call and his boisterous voice filled the room. "Good morning, everybody."

"Morning," the group mumbled in unison.

Coach Creed looked down at Robbie and Sophia and pointed a fat finger at them. "Are you two ready to lead this group of misfits?"

Sophia didn't seem to hear the question. She flipped through a tablet, studying her notes.

Robbie spoke with a distinct Australian accent. "Indeed," he said.

Coach asked, "How's the cold?"

"Much better," said Robbie. "Thanks."

Mr. Benes added, "Probably didn't help that you've been underground for weeks planning for an event like this."

Robbie nodded. "Sophia and I had a feeling that Ms. Günerro would come back to kidnapping large groups of kids, and babies, too. But to be honest we didn't have any idea of the magnitude until yesterday. And now this little baby."

Sophia spoke matter-of-factly. "Yes, Mr. Creed, I do think we are ready. We just have to make sure we have the right team in place to deal with this kind of situation. Now we have Lucas, who will be an invaluable asset."

"Good, good," Coach Creed said. He almost looked

fired up. "We ready, Mr. Benes?"

"I believe so," said Mr. Benes. "We should probably have Emerald take this baby and get her cleaned up."

Emerald immediately popped her head out from the galley. "Yes, sir?" she said, raising her eyebrows.

"Can you take this baby for us?" He coughed and wafted his hand. "I think she needs a diaper change."

Emerald fixed her scarf. "I'd be happy to, sir."

Mr. Benes continued talking to Emerald. "I want you to take care of Gini until we get to Paris, and then I want you to call the ICMEC and tell them we're bringing in an undocumented baby."

"The what?" Emerald asked. "Sorry, I'm new."

"The ICMEC," Sophia said. "The International Centre for Missing and Exploited Children."

Robbie added confidently, "They're the group that originally tipped us off that there might be some large-scale kidnapping—a huge event in Paris."

Sophia said, "It's why we issued a Call to Legs."

"It's why we're going to Paris," said Robbie.

Questions collided in Lucas's brain. He was trying to follow, but he was confused. The Good Company used child labor in factories—but kidnapping? Really? Like selling slaves? And he knew the New Resistance was a group of do-gooders, but breaking up smuggling rings and mass kidnappings was much more than he was prepared for.

"Creed," Mr. Benes said to Coach Creed. "Tell those other Tier One kids to get in here. They're late."

Coach Creed waved his hand in front of the sliding door and it opened with a hiss. Then the four most popular New Resistance members took their time getting to the meeting. Nothing could start without them.

CHILD KIDNAPPING

Travis Chase, a California longboarder with long, wispy blond hair, shuffled into the room. Travis had gone homeless after his parents were killed at the Globe Hotel bombing in Mumbai, India. A year older than Lucas, Travis was already a New Resistance expert on Good Company rules, rituals, and ceremonies, including the dreaded and unblockable Brainwashing Ceremony. He crashed into a seat next to Lucas, unplugged one of his earbuds, and flicked on his tablet.

"'Bout time you made it to the big table," Travis said to Lucas as they slapped hands.

Lucas smiled dryly. "Shut up."

"What's your deal with the baby?"

"I couldn't leave it—her," said Lucas, defending himself. "Why is everybody so, you know, like . . . ?"

"Like . . . ?" Travis said. "It's a Call to Legs, dude."

Lucas clenched his teeth. He didn't feel any smarter sitting at the Tier One table. Sure, it helped having Travis next to him, but he didn't feel heroic or clever or whatever you were supposed to feel at Tier One. And he still didn't get what his dad meant by saying he was "the only one with this kind of firsthand experience." Lucas didn't really remember anything from that experience except maybe an explosion on dark water.

Coach Creed returned to the boardroom followed by three other students.

First was Kerala Dresden, a Swiss high school Goth. At sixteen, she was flawlessly fluent in six languages. However, Kerala's background was sketchy at best. At the age of ten she showed up at the Globe Hotel Luxembourg with black makeup and no history.

Paulo Cabral followed her. The dark-haired fourteen-year-old Brazilian took a seat across from Kerala. Everyone called him "Jackknife" because of his incredible kicks. Lucas and Jackknife had gotten into trouble for playing soccer in the Globe Hotel lobby when Jackknife bent a perfect free kick over Lucas's head. Only problem was that he broke a giant vase they had been using as a goalpost.

That was something Lucas was glad his father had not seen him do.

Next to Jackknife sat Nalini Prasad. At fifteen and wearing an orange *lehenga*, she was an Indian fashion queen. Like Travis, she too had lost her parents in the bombing in Mumbai. Nalini had henna tattoos on her hands and wore an entire jewelry store on her neck, wrists, and ankles. Small bells dangled from her bracelets.

Travis nudged Lucas and muttered to him, "Those

are some hypnotic little chimes."

"Lucas!" Robbie called out, sounding more like a teacher than a teenager. "We need everyone to listen. We have a lot of work to cover this morning."

The entire boardroom got quiet. Coach Creed and Mr. Benes sat in seats on the side. Lucas kept his eyes fixed on Robbie, who would soon be the next youth leader of the New Resistance. If Robbie didn't think you were ready, you would sit on the plane and monitor surveillance cameras with Tier Two.

Being left out was the worst.

"Robbie," said Mr. Benes. "I want to say a word before you and Sophia start." He stood and faced everyone. "Those of you who read this morning's report know that there has been some troubling news about global child labor. Sophia will give you stats in just a minute."

Lucas hoped he could avoid being asked a question about a report he hadn't read. Just like in hotel-school, Astrid's hand shot up first.

"Hang on, Astrid." Mr. Benes gestured toward the front of the room. "Robbie and Sophia are running this mission because using kids, I know, will completely turn the tables on the Good Company. They won't know what to do."

Mr. Benes spoke seriously. "I want you all to know that you are here for a reason. Children are the victims in Ms. Günerro's crimes, so children must be the ones to save them.

"Coach Creed and all New Resistance adults on the plane and in Paris have been instructed to intervene only if it is a life-or-death situation." He paused and then turned his head. "Robbie? Sophia? It's all yours."

There was silence as all eyes shifted back to Robbie and Sophia.

"We're going to watch a few videos today that will give us a close look at what we're up against," Robbie said as he circled the room. "But first, I want Sophia to give the four-one-one on what's what. And, be nice—this is Sophia's first time as meeting leader."

Everyone knew Sophia. She spoke four languages, took only AP classes, and was the newly elected head girl of the New Resistance. Sophia had lost her parents when modern pirates from the Horn of Africa shot and killed them on their yacht off the coast of Somalia. Security was always top of her list.

"I have a few points to make," she said bluntly. "First and most important is safety. If you get into any trouble in Paris, your best bet is to get to the safe house." She paused a beat. "Contrary to conventional thinking, the safe houses located at our three Globe Hotels in Paris will *not* be safe this time around."

A Tier Two kid looked up from his laptop. "Why not?" he asked.

"Because," Sophia continued, "the Good Company will be watching our hotels very closely."

"So where's the safe house in Paris?" Jackknife asked. "Kerala and I have been to the one in India or wherever that was. And that dump in Borneo. But never even been to Paris."

Terry Hines, the Tier Two kid who was now sitting behind Kerala, cut in. "Shakespeare and Company bookshop," he said. "Go there and find Madame Beach. Nice old lady, and her husband cooks great food. Man, I wish I was back on Tier One. Come on, Robbie, let me go to Paris with them."

Robbie puttered his lips at the sandy-haired kid. "Not after the last time, Terry. You went AWOL. You sat in a restaurant and ate curry all day and charged it all on my New Resistance credit card. No way."

Mr. Benes snickered at Robbie.

"That reminds me," said Coach Creed, looking up from his smartphone. "If anybody needs help near Montparnasse, I have some very good Senegalese friends who have an African shop, called Le Gris Gris, on the southeast corner of the train station, located in the middle of rue de l'Ouest—"

"Shakespeare or Le Gris Gris," said Jackknife. "Got it."

Sophia seemed anxious to get on with the meeting and cut Coach off. "Travis?" she asked. "Have you hacked into the Paris security cameras yet?"

"Yeah, yeah," he said, staring at his tablet and shaking his head.

"What's the matter?" Mr. Benes said. "Sorry, Robbie. Not my place."

"It's okay," chuckled Robbie.

"It's just . . ." said Travis. "It's just that it was crazy easy. Like someone had already hacked the system. Easiest hack job I've ever done. It took like sixty seconds with this new app and I could use every street camera in Paris."

"That's great," said Robbie. "So we have access?"

"I've sent an encrypted code to Etta," said Travis. "And she and the Comm Team are already watching the streets of Paris."

"Good," Sophia said, keeping up the pace. "So then what's the Communications Team safety code this time?"

"Orangina," said Travis.

Astrid wrinkled her nose. "The drink?"

"Yes. That's it," said Sophia. "Listen up everyone! Madame Beach is sending a New Resistance agent to meet each of you in Paris. The contact person will have a bottle of Orangina. Once this code is used, it expires for you and your partner. Don't use it again unless you're in trouble. Okay?"

Robbie added, "We will also have Coach Creed in a taxi advertising Orangina."

The airplane hit a pocket of turbulence. Sophia grabbed hold of the table and rattled off her next piece of information.

"A quick update for those who don't read manuals," she said, grinning at Lucas. He fake-smiled back at her. But he also watched the Japanese girl, Sora Kowa, and the other Tier Two kids on the right-hand side closing their laptops. He wasn't alone in not reading boring handouts.

Sophia spoke so fast it was hard to take it all in. "The ILO, the United Nations International Labour Organization, estimates there are more than two hundred million child laborers worldwide. Most kids work in fields, about twenty-five percent in service businesses, and ten percent in factories, making electronics and shoes."

She didn't let up. "The Asia-Pacific and Sub-Saharan Africa regions account for more than two-thirds of this child labor market worldwide. And there are plenty of noteworthy companies using children in their labor forces."

"Let me guess . . ." said Nalini, stopping Sophia's monologue. She shrugged. "The Good Company by any chance?"

"You know," said Kerala, interrupting, "we've done this before. The last time you sent basically this same New Resistance group out, minus Lucas and Astrid, and we all ended up at some circus in Sri Lanka—it wasn't India, Jackknife. And remember we found no microbomb."

"Microbomb." Travis snickered. "Small but deadly."

Jackknife pinched his nose and added, "SBD."

There were a few chuckles from the other kids. Terry thought it was particularly funny and couldn't seem to stop snorting.

The joke aggravated Kerala even more. "Sri Lanka

was awful," she said. "Between the animals almost eating us and those clowns stealing our jewelry, we found no Good Company stolen art, no weapons, no kidnapped kids. Nothing. Everything's a hoax with this company!"

Since he hadn't gone to India or Sri Lanka, Lucas didn't really understand what they were talking about, but he did understand what needed to happen from this point forward.

Lucas looked Kerala right in the eyes. "Just because we've failed before," he said coolly, "doesn't mean we shouldn't try again."

Kerala smacked her gum. She looked like she was going to spit it in Lucas's face.

"Well put, Lucas. Thank you," Sophia said. "You all know I'm a bit heavy on security. We've arranged to have you taken into Paris in metal shipping containers. Don't worry. We've used some of them before. It's safe. You'll have plenty to eat, and you can see out. You will be locked inside and can use your elevator access codes to open the doors."

Sophia tapped on the remote control buttons, and immediately individual monitors descended from the ceiling.

"That's my report," said Sophia with a tiny grin of success. "Now it's showtime!"

Smart boards and table monitors lit up, and everyone leaned in to watch the Good Company movie.

THE IN-FLIGHT MOVIE

Emerald returned to the boardroom, pushing a beverage cart with Gini sitting on top. As Emerald passed out drinks, Gini seemed to be on a parade float, tossing candy and peanut packets onto the table.

Everyone enjoyed Gini's sideshow, Nalini in particular. "Aww," she said, waving a bracelet bell at the toddler. "The baby Gini!"

The monstrous crackle of Cokes and chips and candy wrappers being opened together sounded like a small thunderstorm.

"Ooooh," Gini peeped as she grabbed at Emerald's hand.

Out of the corner of his eye, Lucas noticed—or thought he noticed—a tattoo on Emerald's wrist.

"Quiet down!" Coach Creed bellowed. "It's movie time."

Robbie pointed at a monitor. "I have two videos today that show where we are globally with the Good Company."

A scratchy white snow filled the screens as the boardroom lights dimmed. Robbie talked over the frames, giving a play-by-play. Travis and Lucas each opened a bag of gummy bears and dumped them on the table.

"This clip was stolen by our agents in Waziristan in northwestern Pakistan, where one of our girls' schools was bombed a few years ago."

The film rolled on the screens and almost came into full focus.

A massive dust storm blew in a poor, remote village. A clump of boys between the ages of nine and fourteen was standing awkwardly outside a black bus with tinted windows. The boys were wearing masks. Russian-made Kalashnikov rifles were strapped over their shoulders.

"These boys are known as Curukians," said Robbie. "We have good reason to believe you may meet them in Paris."

"Who are the—" someone in Tier Two started to ask, but the film continued.

While the video ran, Robbie pointed at the woman on the screen. "This is Siba Günerro, president and CEO of the Good Company."

Ms. Günerro ran a gnarled finger through her salt-and-pepper hair. She looked out through her cat-eye sunglasses and clapped her hands rapidly.

The boys then tossed smoke bombs inside an old stucco house. Moments later children in rags ran from the smoke-filled building, and the Curukians dragged them onto a bus. Once the bus was full, Ms. Günerro climbed into the driver's seat and drove off into the desert.

"One thing to note," said Sophia. "This bus is amphibious, meaning that it can travel on land and through water, provided that it is airtight."

Robbie turned up the lights. "That's all we have for video one," he said.

Sophia clicked the remote, which faded the video. The screens filled with a photograph of an African-Asian man with long fingers and perfect fingernails and wearing a furry-hooded parka. Specks of white ice dotted his pores. His smile showed piano-key-perfect teeth.

"This photograph of Mr. Lu Bunguu was taken twelve years ago while on the Good Company's largest ship, the *Lollipop* that often sails in the Argentine sea," said Sophia. "Bunguu, as most people call him, was born in a Good Company refugee camp in Moldova some thirty-five years ago. He truly is a man with no country. He is now looking to buy multilingual children to help stage coups and overthrow governments throughout Asia, Africa, Europe, and the Americas."

Robbie added, "Mr. Bunguu is currently the world leader in child kidnapping."

"Meaning?" Lucas asked. His eyes darted around the room to see if anyone thought his question was stupid. No one said anything.

Sophia clarified. "Meaning that he doesn't kidnap. But that for the last twelve years, he has bought or sold more children than anyone else on the planet."

"He's a child trader," said Travis. "Pun intended."

"What pun?" Kerala said.

"A child trader," Travis explained, "is a child traitor."

Everyone chuckled at Travis's cleverness.

Robbie's voice cut the laughter short. "Bunguu's main supplier of children," he said frankly, "is . . . you guessed it . . ."

Nalini jumped in and answered. "Siba Günerro and the Good Company." She laughed. "Two right for me!"

Sophia's voice cracked as she explained. "Child labor, as many of you know, is rampant in a large swath of the world—from Mauritania in West Africa across the Middle East to Pakistan and down through Indonesia. Kids are enslaved and made to perform all sorts of work against their wills. Some kids don't even get the chance to go to school."

At hearing *no school*, the kids all groaned a collective "whoa," and they began talking about what that meant. Sophia clicked the remote and loaded the next video. The education conversation dimmed with the lights.

At hearing *child brides*, the girls all groaned a collective "ewwwww," and they began talking about it. Sophia clicked the remote and loaded the next video. The child-bride conversation dimmed with the lights.

"Hey, guys! Please stay focused on the monitors," Robbie said. "In Paris, tourist areas are filmed by the Ministry of Security. Travis's hacking job came up with this clip."

Travis smiled. "Actually, our Comm Team spliced this footage with some of our own shots filmed by a Resistance cameraman."

The film jiggled as a cameraman ran through a park. He was breathing hard and there was a sound of crunching feet on a gravel pathway.

"Sorry this footage is a little blurry," Robbie added. "But we didn't want a repeat of last year when our film crew was captured by the Good Company."

The camera stopped and panned. Park benches. Trees. Tourists. The camera focused on a woman in a pair of cat-eye sunglasses that sparkled in the light of the sun.

"Again, this is our friend Ms. Günerro," Robbie explained. "Take a close look."

Ms. Günerro leaned back on the park bench. She looked like an old actress in a long sequin dress, and she smiled haughtily.

Robbie smirked. "This might be the first recorded smile of Ms. Günerro—ever!"

Everyone laughed, as joking seemed to relieve a growing and obvious tension.

Robbie continued. "She's smiling because the Good Company has just reported earning more money than ever before. Their stock is up, and it's mostly because of this guy walking up here: Mr. Charles Magnus, head of the Good Company security division. Mr. Magnus is an ex-cop wanted worldwide for theft, murder, and kidnapping."

The film continued.

Charles Magnus was a stocky, bearded man in his mid-forties. He wore a one-piece green leather uniform, the kind used by racing motorcyclists. There was tons of junk on his belt: a pistol, golden handcuffs, and a mobile phone. He sat next to Ms. Günerro. She blew her nose with a tissue.

"I love this part," said Robbie, interrupting. "Just listen to this cheerful introduction."

"I hate Paris," Ms. Günerro said. "This city is filthy."

She flung the tissue on the ground next to a can of Coca-Cola Light. Ms. Günerro coughed. "There's trash everywhere, and it's full of little French people who don't speak English."

Charles Magnus said, "Well, Siba—Paris is—after all, a French city. It's only natural that the French speak French—in—France."

Over the top of her cat-eye sunglasses, Ms. Günerro glared at Magnus, "Don't get smart with me, Chuckie. I know you're proud these days. You think this new round of kidnappings will bolster profits and our little investors will all be giddy, but don't let it go to your fat head."

"Wonderful people," Robbie mocked as the video briefly paused and skipped, and then restarted.

Astrid added, "The Good Company is anything but."

Charles Magnus said, "My plan will work if we bring in neglected kids from all over. It will be like kidnapping Mexicans in the United States. No one will miss them."

Robbie cut in. "More proof that they are not only criminals but also xenophobic racists."

There was a great burst of outrage at Magnus's comment, and the next moment the room exploded in remarks.

"I hate them."

"They're a dreadful group."

"That's just wrong."

"We shouldn't even have countries."

Even the normally very quiet Sora Kowa spoke up. "What a pity," she said.

Coach Creed boomed, "Quiet!"

Ms. Günerro opened a silver thermos-like canister. A thin white mist curled from its top. She inhaled the vapor, closed the lid, and appeared to calm down. Then she hissed, "Has there been any Resistance?"

"That's us, guys," Robbie interjected.

Charles Magnus said, "There's been chatter. But not to worry. If the New Resistance shows up, I'll have some boys ready to meet them."

Ms. Günerro asked, "Curukians?"

Charles Magnus said, "Yes. I have a few groups mobilizing at the Globe Hotels in Paris. And my A-team took out some New Resistance sympathizers yesterday at the Eiffel Tower. So we know they know something. If it gets out of hand, I have some friends in the Paris police department who owe me a favor or two."

Sophia paused the video on a picture of Charles Magnus rubbing his beard.

"I know I should know this," said Terry, wiping chocolate from his lips. "What . . . what are Curukians again?"

Lucas was relieved that he wasn't the only one who didn't really know.

"Curukians are essentially hired killers," Robbie said. "Most are boys between ten and eighteen years old. The older boys all seem to want to work as Curukian Security. They have zero education and little hope. You can spot them by their black uniforms and their peach-fuzz mustaches."

That confirmed it for Lucas. The boys who had pulled him into the van in the hotel parking lot were Curukians. But possibly double agents of some kind.

Robbie scanned the room for a second and let the information sink in. "Lucas," he asked. "You looked like you were about to say something."

"I'm fine," said Lucas. "Go ahead."

Robbie continued. "Ms. Günerro has scooped up kids in poverty from all over the globe, and she uses them for everything. There are conflicts going on— from Western Sahara to Burma—that have produced entire populations of children who know nothing but fighting.

"So when Ms. Günerro offers a job to these kids, they take it and they'll do anything she asks. They've been known to sew her clothes and clean her toilet.

But they're also suspected of strangling two tourists at the Eiffel Tower yesterday, which is why the tower is closed."

"Excuse me." Astrid sat up. "What exactly is the derivation of the term *Curukians*?"

"That is a very astute question," Sophia said. "Honestly, it's something we don't know and something we hope to find out."

Robbie added, "We've never been able to infiltrate the Good Company or the Curukians at a deep and meaningful level."

The video started rolling again.

In the park there were joggers and businessmen on phones, and an old man loading mules into a truck. The camera zoomed in on Ms. Günerro and Magnus still sitting on the bench.

Ms. Günerro said, "See that boy there?"

She pointed across the park, and the camera panned.

Charles Magnus said, "Yes."

The camera zoomed in on a boy in a Good Company T-shirt skittering around the park like a clumsy spy hiding behind trees and benches.

Ms. Günerro chuckled. "I hired him . . . to steal me a poodle!"

Charles Magnus grinned. "To keep you incognito."

"Yes, but you know I hate dogs as much as . . ."

"Babies?"

"Who doesn't hate babies?" Ms. Günerro rolled her

eyes. "They can't work and they can't make me money."

Charles Magnus cleared his throat. "It would be easier to brainwash babies than teenagers."

"We tried that once, didn't we?" Ms. Günerro asked.

"Yes," he said, "but the nuns in Tierra del Fuego ruined it."

"You still think brainwashing babies is a good idea?" Ms. Günerro said.

Charles Magnus responded deliberately. "I have test groups already working in Egypt, Vancouver, and Seattle."

"You're a good egg, Chuckie," she said. "And then we would have an endless supply of workers—but I still have this order from Bunguu to fill."

"After the carnival," Charles Magnus said, "we will have plenty of well-educated children who won't even know they work for us."

Robbie paused the video.

"Robbie?" Lucas asked. "What does an 'order to fill' mean?"

"We think," said Robbie, "that Bunguu is simply paying Ms. Günerro to kidnap kids for him."

Drinks rattled in the holders as the airplane hit another pocket of turbulent air. The FASTEN YOUR SEAT-BELT light flashed as Captain Bannister broke in over the PA system.

"Sorry about that, folks," he said. "It looks like the city has a few potholes in the road up here! As Etta likes to say, buckle those belts now."

Robbie scrambled back to his seat. "Listen up. This is what we are looking for."

Ms. Günerro chuckled. "Soon . . ."

Charles Magnus grinned as he looked toward the Eiffel Tower. "The French government should not have fired us from guarding the Eiffel Tower in the first place."

"Serves them right," Ms. Günerro said. "If we were guarding that tower, those tourists wouldn't have been killed. . . ."

"Robbie, hold on a second," Mr. Benes said, looking around the room. "I know this is a very confusing company to you all. The Good Company actually has legitimate businesses. My wife used to work for the Good Hotel Bali until she uncovered secret bank accounts and this child-kidnapping ring." Mr. Benes leaned forward and focused on the kids at the table. "Ms. Günerro will appear to do everything in the open, but you never know what's going on behind the scenes. Just do the thing that has the highest value at any given moment, and you'll be making the right choice. Okay?"

Mr. Benes's words flooded Lucas's mind. He had always thought that the Good Company only did bad things. But that was a simple way of looking at the world. Everybody knew that good people sometimes did bad things. Now Lucas realized the inverse was true: Bad people sometimes could actually do good things.

Robbie continued. "This next section of video is why we think she's planning something big."

Charles Magnus said, "Are we ready?"

"Make it happen," Ms. Günerro replied.

Then Charles Magnus pulled out a small silver device and a key card from his coat pocket.

"Watch, closely." Robbie said. "Unfortunately, we can't hear what they are saying because a jet is flying overhead, so we don't know why they have our key card."

Ms. Günerro put the key card into the device. They both looked up at the jet. Then Magnus said something, and Ms. Günerro put the silver box into a shopping bag.

Robbie paused the video and interrupted. "That silver box she's carrying, we believe, is a specialized key-card reader."

Coach stepped up to the main screen behind Robbie. He squinted and pointed at an object.

"What's that sticking out of her shopping bag?" Coach asked.

"We think . . ." said Robbie. He shrugged. "That it's a snorkel."

"A snorkel?" Terry blurted out.

"Yes," said Sophia. "Remember, Ms. Günerro is a certified scuba diver, so it's not unusual for her to have a snorkel, even if it is a bit odd to have one in the middle of Paris. She is a lot of things: She is a concert pianist, and she owns yacht-racing teams and a sports car collection, and she even has an F-16 fighter for fun."

"Awesome," said Terry.

"Back to the video," said Robbie as the film rolled.

Ms. Günerro said, "By that time, they will have all forgotten about their mommies and daddies and everything else in their past. And we, only we, will have access to their brains."

The video stopped, and the monitors went black and slowly receded into the table slots.

Astrid said, "I mean, don't they have police in Paris to do this kind of stuff?"

The edge in Astrid's voice unleashed a flurry of nervous chatter from everyone.

"The police can't find out a thing."

"They're in with Magnus."

"He said so himself."

"Chuckie, you mean."

"They've done nothing wrong, yet."

"There's nothing to prove."

Lucas couldn't keep up with who was talking.

"Typical," said one of the Tier Two guys.

"It's not on their radar."

"We're watching their surveillance cameras."

"And there's nothing."

"Yet."

"It's on *our* radar."

"Of course it is," said Robbie. His voice boomed from the front of the room. "We're the New Resistance."

"But they don't know us," said Lucas.

"They *do* know us," Sophia corrected. "They know the New Resistance, but they *don't* know you, Lucas, or Astrid."

"Remember," said Mr. Benes. "They think you died on that ferryboat."

"Let's get a move on, folks!" Coach Creed roared into the room. "The best defense is a good offense. Everybody back to their regular seats."

It took a few seconds, but most of the kids grabbed their laptops and tablets and headed out of the room and into the other sections as if they were changing classes at hotel-school.

Terry filled his backpack with snacks. Kerala laid her head on the table and fake-slept. The Tier One and Two girls clumped together near Sophia while she gave one last instruction. "The video will be replayed on channel seven on your individual monitors," she said. "Study it frame by frame. Remember! Our primary goal here is to gather information about a possible kidnapping. That's all."

Lucas spotted Gini on the serving cart. Emerald had stopped and seemed to be texting. Lucas was sure you weren't supposed to text on a plane, but he shook it off and caught up with Travis, Jackknife, Terry, and Robbie.

"Kidnapping?" said Terry. "What about that Brainwashing Ceremony? That sounds awesome."

"Dude." Travis stopped the group of guys. "A Brainwashing Ceremony is wicked."

In a tight group, the boys followed Travis into the next compartment. Travis pulled the other earbud out and let it fall to his shoulder. "What would be cool would be to get it on film, you know."

"You told me a long time ago that it was dangerous," said Jackknife.

"That's why I want to film it," said Travis. "From what I've read, Ms. Günerro does some seriously weird things in there. She's got some freaky chant. You know, I actually feel sorry for those Curukians that this happens to. I mean, everybody has bad memories, especially in the New Resistance—"

Jackknife interrupted. "Yeah, but . . ."

"Yeah, but," said Travis, "like Coach Creed always says . . . no matter how bad your past is . . ."

They all nodded and finished the line. "You still don't want it erased."

CURUKIANS

With a mask stretched across his eyes, Lucas slept in his seat pod for the remainder of the flight. A few hours before sunrise on the longest day of the year the plane landed outside a stone village fifty miles south of Paris. There the kids deplaned and went into the small private airport and through an office, where a New Resistance customs officer stamped their passports. Then they climbed two by two into large shipping containers that had been loaded onto the backs of trucks.

The inside of Lucas's shipping container had been converted into a cozy house with a miniature living room and kitchenette and bathroom. Car batteries supplied electricity. Custom-built in Vancouver and modernized with RFID technology, the container was the New Resistance's newest ploy to infiltrate the Good Company.

Astrid sat in the recliner and began reading. Lucas was starved and ready for breakfast, lunch, and dinner. He opened the tiny fridge, microwaved a pizza, and sat on the couch and ate. A few hours later the shipping container slammed down on a loading dock. Lucas peered out a one-way window and watched in horror.

A clump of boys in black—Curukians—pushed through a heavy door and into a warehouse with wooden beams and stone walls. A sign on the wall read GOOD COMPANY PARIS. The five teenagers crossed a loading dock and stopped abruptly as they eyed the enormous metal shipping container.

Through the window Lucas watched the boys approach. He turned on the exterior microphone.

The first boy in line said, "What's this doing here?"

"It's a shipping container," the last boy sneered. "It's *supposed* to be on a loading dock."

"But we had no scheduled shipments today," said the first boy.

"That's weird," said the boy behind him. "This container has the same markings as the one we saw in Vancouver."

"They all look alike," said another.

"Shut up," said the first boy. "What do you know? You lost a baby on that trip."

The boy cracked his neck. "But I made up for it yesterday at the Eiffel Tower."

The first boy opened his backpack, and with his tattooed hands he ripped a piece of duct tape off a roll. He stretched the tape across both doors. A second boy pulled a can of spray paint from under his shirt and tagged the door with big graffiti words.

"Raffish, Curuk," he said as he spray-painted the words over the tape. "That way we'll know next time if we've seen it before."

"Ms. Günerro should know about this," said the first boy. "I'll send our island boys here to keep guard."

Lucas stared through the window, trying to see if he recognized one of the boys from the van. He kept his eyes glued on the Curukians as they disappeared down a long corridor.

A horrible feeling struck him.

Seeing those boys in person had triggered something in him. He felt so out of place, lost—like a new kid thrown into hotel-school. Now he was an outsider—this time in Paris, in another world, a corrupt adult world. Good Company. Bad Company. They all had secrets. He had them too. Everybody had secrets. Everybody. It even made him wonder if the information he'd gotten from the boys in the van was true or not. He swallowed and looked back at Astrid, who was still sitting in the recliner, reading *The History of Kidnapping* in French.

Lucas scanned the inside of the container. His side of the room looked like a herd of goats had been camped out all night. In the few hours that it took to drive from the New Resistance airstrip, Lucas had amassed a pile of pizza boxes, sushi trays, and drink cans. Astrid set her book on the rug, looked at the trash around Lucas's couch, and shook her head.

"That's nasty," Astrid said.

She shuffled to the front and typed a code into a reader. With a bleep, the electronic bolt on the shipping container unlocked. The duct tape held the doors closed for a second, and then—*snap!*—the tape split and the doors opened.

With a severe case of bed head, Lucas stepped out of the container and onto a loading dock.

"My hair hurts," he said, rubbing his head.

"Looks great!" Astrid said.

He grinned. "I worked on it all night."

To his left, stone walls formed a long corridor. "Let's find out where those boys went," said Lucas, moving toward a flickering light.

Banks of fluorescent lights along the ceiling buzzed and blinked off and on. Water dripped from the ceiling, making the walls damp and the air musty. Stacked along the sidewalls, rusted barricades leaned haphazardly on one another. There were coils of hoses and cables and wire everywhere.

"What's that mean?" Lucas asked, reading a sign on a door. "*Sans issue* in French means what? 'Without issue'?"

"No." Astrid crinkled her nose. "*Sans issue* means 'no exit.'"

"I thought there was another way to say 'no exit.'"

"Doesn't matter," said Astrid. "It's not a good sign for us."

Someone banged on a metal door. Lucas's eyes popped wide open. Astrid froze. The door slammed closed and the corridor lights went out as someone muttered something in the dark. They crouched behind their shipping container in a nest of old telephone wires.

From the hallway came the sounds of someone shuffling around. The person tripped over some sort of pipe, and it fell to the stone floor with a clatter. The lights went off and then came on again, followed by the clump of a cane.

A moment later a bald-headed boy wearing a faded Zidane soccer shirt limped into the room. He held a wooden cane in one hand, a newspaper under his arm, and an Orangina in his other hand.

The boy spoke English with a very strong French accent. "Is there someone?" Then in French he said the same thing. *"Il y a quelqu'un?"*

Lucas and Astrid stayed in the shadows and watched.

"Listen," said the boy. He tossed the Orangina in the air like a ball. "I am calling myself Hervé Piveyfinaus, and I work with the New *Résistance*."

. Lucas followed Astrid as she slowly inched out of the shadow.

"Bonjour," said the French boy as he kissed Astrid on both cheeks and shook hands with Lucas.

Astrid blushed but got straight to the point. "So, Hervé," she said. "You have an Orangina."

"But of course," said Hervé.

Several things were bothering Lucas at that moment.

Top of his list was Gini. Where was she, and how

would the ICMEC get her back to her parents in Egypt? Was she really Egyptian? And why had he promised to get her home?

The second thing that didn't seem right was this French boy standing in front of them. Yes, he had an Orangina bottle, which meant he had gotten Travis's code. But there was something that Lucas just didn't trust. Maybe it was the accent or the cane or possibly the bald head. He scratched sleep from his eyes and spoke without thinking.

"What's the deal . . . with the cane, I mean?" he blurted, his tone harsher than he had intended. "And you're bald. No offense, but like, how old are you? A bald-headed kid with a cane is um . . . not what I was expecting."

Astrid shot him a sidelong look. "Lucas!"

"I have seventeen years," said Hervé. "And I have leukemia, the cancer, and for that I have chemotherapy and it makes me bald. For my leg, I am having surgery for the bone marrow."

The French boy lifted his pant leg and showed a nasty burned scar on his calf. The muscle was largely missing, and his skin looked like bark on a dying tree.

"I'm sorry," said Lucas. "My bad." Still, Lucas wasn't completely sold on Hervé. He was hiding something.

"My brother's a little . . ." Astrid offered with a roll of her eyes. "I don't know—jet-lagged."

"It is okay," said Hervé. He leaned on his cane. "I am coming to meet you today because . . ." He glanced over his shoulder. "Madame Günerro, *président* of the Good Company, is arriving in moments, and the paparazzi will meet her outside the hotel. This is where we hope to learn of her plans."

"*Madame* Günerro?" Astrid asked. "Is she married?"

"I doubt it," said Hervé. "I called her *madame* because she is old."

Outside the heavy doors where the Curukians had entered the warehouse, a faint siren screeched *beedoo, beedoo,* and the sound bleated louder then softer as the cars passed.

"But of course," said Hervé in a serious tone. "This must be her police escort."

From the dark corridor there came another burst of noise, metal pipes clanging and a rattling and jiggling on the doorknob. Then somebody kicked a door open, and the sound blasted down the hallway.

"Apparently we have already Curukians," said Hervé hurriedly. "Island boys . . . here to talk then fight."

"What?" Lucas said.

"Robbie explained all this." Astrid glared at her brother. "You need to listen."

"It's not that," said Lucas. "I just don't believe everything I hear, especially when it's so . . ."

"Believe this," said Hervé. "I am prepared to take revenge on Curukians for what they have done to me."

This was all just too perfect for Lucas. He felt like he and Astrid were being set up.

The boys in the corridor seemed to be arguing. Somebody knocked at a door, and it opened and then slammed closed. There was a slap. Then another slap and a crash into the metal barricades.

The three Curukians were still arguing in what sounded like gibberish when they came into the light. They looked similar to the boys in the Waziristan video on the plane, a little overweight, in their mid-teens at best. Their thin peach-fuzz mustaches looked like dirt under their noses. Their "uniforms" were all black—boots, pants, and mock turtleneck shirts with a Good Company logo on the front.

The first boy spoke to Hervé in English with a strange accent. "Still trying to help, eh, Hervé?"

Hervé pulled his cane to his leg. "Better than beating you again in a boxing ring, Andry. Nobody in your Madagascar orphanage knows how to box."

The second Curukian boy shrugged. "Why not come back and help us, Hervé?" He folded his arms, swelling his biceps. "You will never make money in the New Resistance."

Lucas knew he had been right about Hervé. The French boy wasn't authentic New Resistance. He knew these Curukian guys.

"No thank you," said Hervé. He glanced at Lucas and Astrid. "These boys will all tell you they are from Raffish, Curuk, but Tahitoa here is actually from Tahiti and he doesn't know what we have in the New *Résistance*."

Now Lucas was really confused. Was Hervé some sort of double agent?

"What?" Andry said. "Them two little kids?"

"We do not care about them," said Tahitoa. "These kids are weak."

As if to prove his point, Tahitoa walked straight up to Lucas and towered over him. Then he spat in Lucas's face. Lucas cringed and thought about saying something clever but decided against it. With his forearm he wiped the slobber from his cheek.

This clearly was not a drill. For a split second the thought crossed his mind to run. But he stayed put. Eventually, he knew, he would have to stand his ground.

Andry's phone chirped with a text.

"Madame Günerro is walking to her hotel for a press conference. Ha. She just got another baby," he said, showing the text to the third Curukian boy. "Maybe we should take these babies to Madame Günerro too."

As he spoke, Andry grabbed Lucas's arm.

Lucas's heart gave a painful jolt. He shook his arm free and took a step backward. The Malagasy boy then pushed him with both arms, and Lucas dropped to the ground. The three Curukian boys fist-bumped each other and laughed, apparently at how easy this was.

For Lucas, the floor was exactly where he wanted to be.

The boy who hadn't spoken yet couldn't stop laughing at Lucas. "Yeah," he snorted. "Take them back with us. That way we can find out if we know if they know what we think we know they think we know."

Nobody seemed to understand him, but Andry and Tahitoa acted like they did and kept laughing.

"You so funny, Ukkuwa," said the other island boys.

Tahitoa then approached Astrid. He looked like he was going to slap her in the face. But she backed up before he could get too close.

"Hey, pretty," he said. "Why you not come with us?"

"Thanks, guys," said Astrid, taking another step back. "I really appreciate it, but Hervé and I already have plans."

While Tahitoa had been harassing Astrid, Lucas had been crawling toward Hervé. Andry spotted Lucas moving around. "Look at the little baby," he said.

Still crouching, Lucas kept his head low.

The boy called Ukkuwa prepared to place a fat boot into Lucas's rib cage.

Lucas's response was a surprise even to himself. From the ground he snap-kicked Ukkuwa in the chest, knocking him back into the other two boys. "Tss," hissed Lucas as he jumped to his feet. He snatched Hervé's cane and blasted out in a whirlwind of motion. The first true drops of adrenaline seeped into his blood. He landed two quick hook punches on Andry and Tahitoa. Looking a little shocked, all three Curukian boys backed up.

Protecting her face and chest, Astrid jumped into

a guarded position behind her brother. The boys moved in. In the next half second Hervé launched his newspaper into Ukkuwa's face. It was a great move. The flying paper completely threw the boy off, and he swatted at it awkwardly.

Lucas spun backward. He flapped the cane behind his head—left, right—slapping the other two boys behind him in the faces. They ran at Lucas. But his arms came sliding back behind him. His elbows nailed them in the guts, knocking the breath out of them.

For Andry the impact seemed so sudden that he dropped to the ground without uttering a sound. Tahitoa scrambled to his knees. Slowly the Tahitian pulled a blade from his sock and jabbed at Hervé with it.

With one snap of her wrist Astrid ridge-punched the Tahitian in the temple. Tahitoa nearly fainted. He pulled both arms around his head and let go of the blade. Lucas dropped to the floor, spun, and back-kicked the boy in the chest. That was it. Tahitoa slumped, writhing, into a fetal position on the ground.

Ukkuwa threw his entire body weight at Hervé. Astrid gave Lucas a hand up. Instinctively Lucas grabbed the cane and pointed it at Ukkuwa. Lucas stepped back, casting the cane into the air like a fly rod, an extension of his own arm. The crook end of the cane hooked around Ukkuwa's legs. Lucas flipped the boy to the ground in one jerk motion. The boy's head hit the cobblestone flat.

Lucas tossed the cane back to Hervé, and they all

looked at the three moaning boys.

"Welcome," said Hervé. "Welcome to the . . . New *Résistance*."

Ukkuwa lifted his head. "Madame Günerro says you will never remember."

Fire lit in Hervé's eyes. He jerked his head toward the boy and quickly snatched up the blade. He pounded on top of Ukkuwa's chest. Then with both hands he raised the knife and aimed it at Ukkuwa's throat.

"I am starting to remember," said Hervé.

Hervé grunted as he pumped the knife twice above his head. Ukkuwa squirmed. But Hervé dug his knees deep into the boy's shoulders. Astrid screamed at what was about to happen. In one single motion Lucas dove across the concrete floor.

Hervé pumped the knife a third time as Lucas's shoulder connected with Hervé's armpit. The knife came down. The blade twisted and moved away from Ukkuwa's throat, nearly nicking his face. Lucas slapped Hervé's forearm, and the knife broke free, skittering across the floor as the three boys crumbled into a pile.

"You can't kill them," Lucas said to Hervé. "They don't know what they're doing—they're probably brainwashed and kidnapped."

"Sri Lanka," said Ukkuwa. "That's my home, my real home, not Raffish—the one they make us say we're from." Then the boy buried his head in his lap and started to sob. "I should have been brainwashed completely, like all the others. It would be easier not to remember anything."

Lucas partly believed the boy and wanted to help him. But now was not the right time.

"I'm sorry," Lucas said flatly. He looked to Astrid. "I need rope."

In a flash Astrid scooped up a clump of telephone wire and tossed it to her brother. Seconds later Lucas had shown he was a true knot master. He tied a killer set of bowline knots on Andry and Tahitoa and roped their legs and arms like they were calves in a rodeo. With a series of hitches, Lucas lashed Ukkuwa to a barricade.

"Let's get out of here," he said.

"Wait," said Hervé, who was still sitting on the ground.

Lucas glanced back at the French boy and then nudged Astrid. With both palms on the door, he pushed through to the outside. What he saw was not at all what he had expected.

WHO'S WATCHING WHOM?

With the memory of the fight swirling in his head, Lucas felt like everything had just become extremely important. He began to wonder if even the smallest clue might have some great meaning. His internal GPS enabled itself, and Lucas began to catalog everything he could see, smell, or hear.

Spread out in front of Lucas and Astrid was a wide cobblestone street filled with tiny cars zipping around like bugs on water. The air smelled of diesel fuel and fresh bread. Across the street, metal scaffolding covered a building where workers were whitewashing walls. Mist and dust showered the street. On the sidewalk, cafés were packed with people sitting in chairs, reading and talking and drinking coffee.

A black bus with tinted windows barreled through the traffic. Lucas noticed that the safety hatch on the roof was broken. Two white vans with no side windows followed the bus. Small satellite dishes shaped like a human ear and eyeball slowly spun on top of each van. In French and in English, the logo and tagline on the sides of the vans said it all:

CHAPTER ELEVEN

GOOD COMPANY IMAGES
WATCHING AND LISTENING
SO YOU DON'T HAVE TO

Lucas's eyes followed the bus and vans down the street until he lost them in the traffic circle. Next to this roundabout there was a Ferris wheel, some carnival-type booths, and a guillotine.

"Weird," Lucas muttered as he looked up.

Directly above his head a security camera scanned the street.

Astrid seemed to be eyeing something completely different. She almost looked dreamy.

"Paris!" she said as if on vacation. "I love it already."

Across the street, clustered together, were the biggest names in French fashion: Chanel, Dior, Louis Vuitton, Hermès, Yves Saint Laurent, Givenchy.

Astrid stepped farther onto the sidewalk, nearly putting her foot in water that was flowing along the curb. "France is so great," she said as if falling in love. "There's a whole Chanel store! That's what mom used to wear. I love that perfume. I love—"

"You're such a girl."

"I *am* a girl. Thank you very much!"

Astrid turned and read a sign on the door. "This is a delivery entrance for the Good Company warehouse," she said. "You're the one with a map of Paris in your head. What's the quickest way to Ms. Günerro's hotel?"

In his mind Lucas brought up a map of Paris. "It's

all the way on the other side of this block." He paused, then pointed. "Go straight five hundred meters toward that Ferris wheel. At those white booths turn east—left. That street should be rue de Rivoli."

Astrid marched ahead of Lucas and down the sidewalk.

"Hey, Astrid," said Lucas as he caught up. "What did that Ukkuwa kid mean by 'you will never remember'?"

"I don't know." She shook her head. "Dad says your mind never really forgets anything."

"Ukkuwa sure did make Hervé mad," he said. "You think Hervé would have really stabbed him? Like really killed him?"

"I don't know," she said. "I thought there was something about Hervé that—"

"You're not going to say cute, are you?" Lucas scrunched his nose.

"I was going to say," said Astrid, "sweet and sad at the same time."

"A double-crosser is not sweet."

"He's helping us," Astrid said. "And no, I didn't read that. I just get it."

"I have a sense about him too," Lucas said defensively. "Just because my feeling is different from yours doesn't mean it's wrong."

"We'll test your theory," said Astrid. "Here he comes now."

Hervé was hobbling quickly down the sidewalk. The French boy raised his cane. "Wait!" he called out.

"Whatever," said Lucas, crinkling an eyebrow. "I'd rather go ride that Ferris wheel than deal with him."

"You act like such a thirteen-year-old," said Astrid.

"I am a . . ." Lucas stalled for a second. "Wait! I am fourteen. Today's my birthday."

"I completely forgot." Astrid swallowed. "It is. Wow. This is kind of weird: Paris on your fourteenth birthday while tracking a kidnapping ring?" She cringed. "That's different."

"Yep."

"We're having a party when we get back," she said. "Just don't get kidnapped."

"Ha-ha."

"Happy birthday," she said. "Honest."

"Thanks," said Lucas. He knew Astrid had a nice side. It just took her forever to get there.

They stopped for a second in front of a bakery to wait for Hervé. Lucas watched the Ferris wheel and calculated the wheel's fractional revolutions per second. He kept getting distracted by a boy who was flapping his arms in front of the guillotine—the famous head chopper-offer from the French Revolution. The mini exhibit was a cardboard replica, and it seemed completely out of place—like a bad Halloween display.

Astrid shook her head at Lucas. "We are *not* doing that—even if it is your birthday."

Hervé panted as he finally caught up with Lucas and Astrid. "Have you waved to the *caméra*?"

"What camera?" Lucas said.

"The security *caméra*," said Hervé.

"You mean," said Astrid, "the security camera that Travis hacked into?"

Lucas opened his eyes wide. "I don't think you're supposed to be talking about that."

"Hervé's with us, Lucas."

"But of course." The French boy pointed across the street. "See that *caméra* on the ministry building? Look at it and wave so that those watching know you are arrived."

Astrid waved at the camera and slapped Lucas for not waving. Lucas raised a reluctant hand toward the camera and noticed that Hervé Piveyfinaus was on the move toward the guillotine.

The smell of chocolate was too tempting. Lucas's eyes drifted to the cakes and pies in the bakery window. He even thought about buying something to eat with the money he had borrowed from his father's change bowl.

"We just ate in the shipping container," said Astrid. "You must have worms."

"I don't have worms," said Lucas. "I like sweet things."

"You're always trying to get out of doing everything."

Lucas lowered his voice. "Hervé is annoying me."

"I think you're wrong about him."

Lucas explained his point of view. "Hervé knew those Curukians—by name. And 'wave at the camera'?

What does that mean? I don't believe this guy, Astrid. I mean come on. The Curukians just so happen to pass in front of our shipping container and then all of a sudden Hervé shows up?"

"You're worrying," she said. "The Orangina code was sent to all New Resistance agents in Paris. It's part of a plan."

"There is such a thing as a double agent." Lucas's face tightened. "I bet he's not telling us something."

"*Mon ami,* my friend. Why the worry face?" Hervé said, rejoining them. "France is not a dangerous place."

"Guillotine!" Guillotine Boy screeched as he let the cardboard "blade" drop. He cried out, "Marie Antoinette, Louis Says, Simon Says."

"The guillotine is not dangerous?" Lucas said.

"Well . . ." said Hervé. "Uh . . ."

Guillotine Boy yelled into the street. "The blade is cardboard," he said in a bad fake French accent. "So you get the sensation of . . . *whack!* . . . without the blood."

"This is awful," said Astrid. "Don't let Kerala see this."

Lucas all of a sudden recognized Guillotine Boy as the poodle thief in the video they had seen on the plane. Before he could explain it to Astrid, she was already showing Hervé a handwritten sign on the wall. It read, *Carnival tomorrow night @ the Eiffel Tower. Free Admission.*

For Lucas there were just too many coincidences,

like it had all been staged.

Maybe, he thought, *everything* has *been staged.*

"Which way?" Astrid said to Lucas. "We need to get to the Good Hotel and see what Ms. Günerro is up to."

Lucas now led his sister through crowded city streets toward the front entrance of the Good Hotel Paris. He walked fast, hoping to lose Hervé along the way. But at the next corner he stopped cold. His jaw dropped as he pointed toward the horizon. The most famous man-made structure in the world towered above the Parisian skyline.

The Eiffel Tower.

They gawked at the sight for what seemed like a very long time. Hervé caught up with them, and Lucas was immediately on the move again. He was determined to shake the French kid until he knew what Hervé was really about. Around another corner, Lucas walked as fast as he could through the thick summer crowd. They zipped past a line of parked cars and ran smack into a wall of people. Shoppers. Tourists. Parisians and Londoners, Arabs and Thais. An ambulance made it seem even more chaotic as its siren screeched down the street.

Then the strangest thing happened. At the Café l'Abri, a boy with thin arms appeared almost out of nowhere. He seemed nervous, wiggling his thin peach-fuzz mustache as if he had a nose itch. From behind his back he pulled an orange and offered it to Astrid.

Lucas cut a sharp eye to his sister. They kept moving without paying the boy any attention. It didn't really make sense. Something was up.

"Okay, that's a little weird," she said. "How did that kid get the code?"

"The almost-correct code," Lucas said.

"I'm already ready to get to the safe house and find out what's really going on."

"I think we've lost Hervé," said Lucas as he sped up his walk. "But let's keep going."

Astrid followed Lucas as he weaved along the crowded sidewalk, past an African couple looking at diamonds, and under a ladder on rue de l'Échelle. Lucas wiggled around the crowd and stood across the street from the front entrance of the Good Hotel Paris. Then he spotted her.

Siba Günerro.

She was dressed like Hollywood royalty in black cat-eye sunglasses and a long white gown that sparkled with sequins. Walking next to her, a poodle dressed with tufts of fluffy pink fur on its legs and tail pulled on its leash. Ms. Günerro rose with purpose up the steps of her Good Hotel Paris. On her hip she held Gini.

Lucas didn't even look for traffic as he started to run across the street to get Gini. Astrid screamed and grabbed his arm just before he stepped in front of a taxi.

Back on the curb Lucas felt a deep headache. Nothing ever really made sense to him. Like how could Ms. Günerro, some supposedly wicked CEO, have Gini, who had just been on White Bird One?

From the top step of the Good Hotel Paris, Siba Günerro, president of the Good Company, turned and spoke to a large crowd of international reporters.

Correspondents clamored to get questions in and paparazzi raised cameras above the crowd, taking rapid-fire pictures. In the middle of the group, Lucas spotted Jackknife. Within seconds he and Astrid crossed the street and mingled with the clump of reporters, right next to Jackknife.

"The news is just dreadful," said Ms. Günerro, her chin tilted slightly upward. "Tourists killed at the Eiffel Tower? I am appalled. It is a tragedy. I do know, however, that had the Good Company been guarding the tower, this would never have happened. The Good Company no longer has a contract to guard that eyeful of an icon. Blame the French government for breaking a deal with us and thus endangering tourists."

Journalists blasted Ms. Günerro with a barrage of questions.

"Madame Günerro? Is the baby yours or from one of your Good Orphanages?" "What is the forecast for company profits?" "What is the fate of the Good Carnival charity event you have planned at the Eiffel Tower?" "What—"

"Everyone knows that I love children—especially babies," said Ms. Günerro with the authority of a detention principal. She spoke sternly as she clicked through the questions. "This wonderful child will be our first child at my favorite new charity, the brand new Good Orphanage Paris.

"Second question: The forecast for profits . . . is *good*." She chuckled. "Very good.

"Third. Our Good Bus keeps helping kids all over the world, and our charity event at the Eiffel Tower is on as planned. You're all invited. And don't be worried. It will be safe. Mr. Magnus and Good Company Security will provide top-shelf security for the event. No French police will be necessary."

"Madame Günerro?" a reporter called from the back of the throng. "Can you speak to the allegations that your company uses child labor?"

"Always one of you in the crowd," she said smugly. "Same answer as last time: preposterous! We're called the Good Company for a reason. We do all things good."

Ms. Günerro stared at Gini proudly. Lucas couldn't believe this person.

"Let me add, from the bottom of my heart . . ." She paused. "The most dreadful thing in our world is a bored child, which is why we take kids, disadvantaged children, and educate them at our Good Schools. This way they can become productive members of our company, of our society."

Another reporter asked a question about nuclear waste, but Ms. Günerro had already turned to enter the hotel. At the top step she turned back and faced the crowd one more time and gave a glitzy smile. The cameras went crazy, which aggravated Lucas even more. Ms. Günerro walked through the revolving doors and into the hotel.

The porters, dressed in red coats and top hats, locked arms and blocked the group of reporters from entering the hotel. Lucas, Astrid, and Jackknife wiggled past the porters and paparazzi, completely unnoticed, and shot up the carpeted flight of stairs.

The pads at the bottoms of the golden revolving glass doors rubbed the ground as they spun around in slow automated circles. The kids stepped inside the lobby of the fancy hotel. What they saw was beautiful; what they heard was horrendous.

THE POINT OF NO RETURN

The hotel lobby was elegant and luxurious with its flower arrangements and candelabras and velvet chairs—a place fit for a king. Yet for some reason the fancy hotel lobby wasn't air-conditioned. Humid summer air was starting to stick to everything. Guests came and went almost in slow motion, babbling in every language.

The terrible noise that Lucas, Astrid, and Jackknife heard came from an alcove on the side of the lobby. Two Curukians with thin, tattooed arms sat at a grand piano, butchering a version of what seemed like "Heart and Soul." The five Curukians who Lucas had seen earlier on the loading dock were now slouching on couches around the piano.

In front of these boys, Ms. Günerro stood and fanned herself with a copy of the magazine *Antarctic Fashion*. Her poodle in pink spun in circles, dragging its leash on the marble floor. Under the piano Gini sat in a stroller and hiccupped in the pauses of the song.

Ms. Günerro then sat next to the boys at the piano and completely surprised everyone. She not only played with flair, but the music was so beautiful that the entire lobby seemed to feel lighter and happier. Everyone was smiling.

"Oh," said Jackknife. "Mr. Siloti had me practicing that song last week."

Astrid added, "That's Beethoven's 'Appassionata.'"

"Yeah," said Jackknife. "But she's good. Really good."

Lucas shook free from his confusion about this wicked woman playing beautiful music. He surveyed the lobby and calculated a plan to get Gini back.

A clattering sound startled him as a porter pushed a wobbly-wheeled luggage cart across the tiled floor. Behind the cart a French family followed, pulling French suitcases made in China by the Good Company.

As soon as the cart had passed, the last person Lucas wanted to see appeared in front of them.

"Hervé!" Astrid said. "Where did you just come from?"

The bald-headed French boy panted. "Lucas is good at losing people." He grinned. "I am good at finding them, which is why Madame Beach sent me to meet you."

Lucas couldn't put his finger on what was bothering him about Hervé, but he felt like Hervé just wasn't being completely truthful. Whatever the reason, Lucas felt like he had wasted enough time. "I'm going to get Gini back."

"What?" Jackknife asked, scrunching his thick black eyebrows. "What are you going to do?"

"I don't know," said Lucas. "I'm just going to go and take her back."

"I am confounded by this," Hervé said, still breathing hard. "You must not confront Madame Günerro. This, I know."

"You seem to know a lot," said Astrid.

"About them," said Lucas, pointing at Ms. Günerro and her Curukians.

Hervé glanced back at Ms. Günerro and then leaned on his cane and hung his head as if to hide. "I know too much, unhappily."

Lucas was about to strangle this kid. "Well then tell us what you know!"

"But of course," said Hervé.

"Like," said Astrid, "how did Ms. Günerro get Gini off our plane?"

Hervé shrugged. "This I do not know."

"I can tell you that," said Jackknife.

The three kids looked at Jackknife.

"This is like my fifth Tier One mission with the New Resistance," he said. "But I have never seen so many things go wrong. Maybe it's because grown-ups are not in charge."

Astrid leaned over Lucas's shoulder and closed the circle so they could listen to Jackknife's story.

"So anyway," he continued. "You both left in your storage container. And all the others were loaded onto the trucks, and they all took off to different parts of Paris. No problem. But the ground crew had trouble with my container. So Kerala and I had to wait in the little airport café. She ran back into the airplane to do something. Fix that beautiful black makeup, I'm sure. And then there was this rush of cars, like customs agents or passport agents, I thought, only they were unmarked SUVs with tinted windows, and they surrounded our plane."

"Aha," said Hervé. "The Gooder Guard."

"Gooder Guard?" Lucas asked.

Hervé nodded. "That's what we used to call them."

"So you know them?" Astrid asked.

"No, no," said Hervé. "They know me."

Lucas spoke to Jackknife. "Go on," he said.

Jackknife continued. "These guys, they were more like Iraqi Republican Guards wearing those dumb-looking crash helmets. But they said they were with the ICMEC and they were there to get a baby. Two seconds later they rushed onto White Bird One. It was crazy. A minute or two later they left the airplane with Emerald and the baby and got into their SUVs. And they drove away."

"What about my dad?" Lucas asked.

"And Coach Creed?" Astrid added.

Jackknife kept talking. "And Robbie and Sophia and all the others, too," he said. "Supposedly Kerala had been in a bathroom when all this was going on. She said that she had smelled something electrical burning."

"On the plane?" Lucas said.

Jackknife nodded. "Yeah."

"So . . ." Lucas said with wide eyes. "Were they in there? Are they . . ."

"I don't know," said Jackknife. "Kerala didn't see or hear anyone on the plane because the electronic lock on the boardroom door had been destroyed and she couldn't open it. She doesn't know what happened, except something was burning."

"So then what?" Astrid asked.

"After the Gooder Guard took Emerald and Gini, Kerala ran out and got in our container, which was already on the truck. The driver didn't seem to know anything. He just took us into Paris—to a warehouse on the other side of the Seine. We crossed the river back to this side, and as soon as Kerala saw Ms. Günerro and the reporters outside the hotel, she took off on her own."

Hervé stuck his bald head between Lucas and Astrid. "Believe me," he said. "Madame Günerro, she has her ways. Kerala is smart. We must avoid this woman. I am telling you I know she has ways of making anyone do what she wants."

Lucas stepped into the middle of the crowded lobby and tried to think. For him, algebra made sense—he could always solve for x. In this case there was no x marking the spot. Everything in his mind was cluttered. Even the languages he could hear around him were confusing: Chinese mixing with Khmer and Arabic and Dutch. All the schooling he had had in his life had not prepared him for a time when things were as vague and puzzling as they were now. Everything seemed to have fallen apart so quickly. They were truly on their own.

The others joined Lucas under the chandelier. Astrid declared, "I think it's pretty clear that something's not right here. We should probably go to the safe house."

"Where is this found?" Hervé asked.

Lucas ignored Hervé. "You're right," he said to Astrid. "The *smart* thing to do is go to the safe house. That's what we're supposed to do. But the *right* thing to do—is find Gini."

MASTER KEY, MASTER PLAN

Lucas, Astrid, Jackknife, and Hervé stood motionless under the chandelier in the center of the crowded lobby. To the left, Ms. Günerro still mesmerized everyone with her beautiful piano playing. On the opposite side, the café was packed, and waiters bustled noisily back and forth to the tables. From behind the reservations desk, Charles Magnus emerged and marched into the hotel's lobby.

The big bearded man walked right past Lucas and his group. Hervé hunched over and hid his face. Magnus stopped at the lobby café and spoke to two security guards who were drinking coffee and eating beignets covered in powdered sugar. Magnus then cut back across the lobby and approached Ms. Günerro.

Hervé turned his back and whispered, "That's Charles Magnus, head of Good Company Security."

"We know," said Jackknife. "We saw a video."

Lucas snapped, "What video did *you* see, Hervé?"

"I know you do not have confidence in me, Lucas," said Hervé, almost pleading. "I am trying to help you. Honest."

Ms. Günerro was still seated at the piano. She

finished her tune in dramatic fashion and most everyone in the lobby and café applauded. Charles Magnus whispered into his boss's ear as two boys next to Ms. Günerro began slapping at the piano keys. Ms. Günerro's expression changed. She stood and closed the piano on the boys' fingers. With a flip of her wrist, Ms. Günerro shooed them all out the front door.

Magnus took the poodle by the leash while Ms. Günerro pushed Gini in the stroller. They pretended to be some happy family, which made Lucas even madder. The fake family strolled down a far hallway with their baby and dog, and they got on an elevator and disappeared.

"Great," said Lucas, throwing his hands up. "We have no idea where they went."

"Probably," said Hervé, "to the office."

"What office?" Astrid said.

"In each Good Hotel," Hervé explained, "Madame has an office, a room to which she diverts all the air conditioning."

Jackknife said bluntly, "Well where is it?"

"Nobody knows," said Hervé. "It can change from day to day. She is nervous, no?"

Astrid was persistent. "We really should go to the safe house."

"No," said Jackknife. "Lucas is right. We should get the little girl. We've got time because Magnus obviously doesn't know us."

"He knows me," said Hervé.

Lucas folded his arms. "You're not telling us the whole story," he said. "Are you?"

"No," said Hervé. "I am not. But you know how it feels when no one believes you. You eventually stop telling the whole truth, and you come to rely only on yourself because you know what you are doing is right."

For the moment that made sense to Lucas, and he nodded deeply. Hervé *was* actually helping; he was just different.

Astrid sighed. "So what's the plan, guys?"

"Just get a master key card," said Jackknife. "We'll find them."

"Just like that?" Lucas asked."

"I get them all the time," Astrid said confidently. "We'll get Gini and then go to the safe house. Deal?"

The boys agreed.

"What are you going to do?" Jackknife asked. "Just ask for a French key card?"

The grin on Astrid's face bordered on evil. "I know exactly what I'm going to do." Astrid gathered her hair behind her. "How does my hair look?"

"Terrible," said Lucas.

"Your hair looks very . . . nice," Hervé said hesitantly. "I do speak French. Do you want that I come with you?"

"You boys can watch," Astrid said with a self-righteous snicker. "But I got this."

Hervé, Lucas, and Jackknife followed Astrid to the

reservations counter. It was at this point that Lucas actually started to get worried. If the Good Company knew Hervé, then Ms. Günerro and Magnus would soon find anyone with him.

The tall blond teenager behind the counter was no more than sixteen years old. He smiled at Astrid and then spoke rapidly. "Hello. *Bonjour.*"

On his shirt a name tag read BOUTROS SVENGALVIK. Below his name were French, Russian, Swedish, and British flags, indicating the languages he spoke. He was dressed in a French blue shirt and tie, and when he spoke, his nose curled, making it even more pointed. The French and English that came from his mouth were both lightning fast.

He said, "Can I help you? *Est-ce que je peux vous aider?*"

"We—we need a key to our room," stammered Astrid in English and then in fast French. *"Nous avons besoin d'une clé pour notre chambre."*

Boutros lightly poised his fingertips on a keyboard. "Did you receive a card already?"

Astrid pulled a Globe Hotel key card from her pocket. "This one doesn't work."

Boutros took her key card and examined it. "This belongs to the Globe Hotel," he said. "This is the *Good* Hotel. Our cards are slightly different. Perhaps you are mistaken."

Boutros swiped Astrid's Globe Hotel key card into a reader and set it on the counter. His look was puzzled and almost desperate as he stared at his monitor. He typed furiously on the keyboard.

"Strange," he said. "This card for some reason has security access for our buses. We must have a bug in our system. Of what means did you obtain this card?"

"Uh," Astrid said softly. "My uncle gave it to me."

"Your uncle?"

"Uncle Magnus," said Astrid.

Good one, Lucas thought.

"Oh," said Boutros. "His niece!" Boutros scratched his head and looked at the four teenagers standing before him. His eyebrows buckled as he focused on Hervé. "Do we know each other?"

Hervé said, "Perchance."

Lucas and Jackknife eyed each other. Then Lucas spun around and took stock of the lobby. It was still very busy. The two security guards who had been in the café were eating what appeared to be another plate of beignets. There was now powdered sugar everywhere around them—on the floor, the table, and their dark blue jackets.

Astrid gathered her hair and swept it around so that it fell across her shoulder. "May I call you Boutros?" she asked in a breathy tone.

Boutros leaned in closer to Astrid and spoke so softly Lucas could not hear at all.

Astrid kept spinning her magic and pointed at the flags on his jacket. "Do you really speak all those languages?"

"I do," said Boutros, now resting his elbows on the counter. "Your French is quite good. Do you speak other languages?"

"I speak English, obviously," said Astrid. "And French and okay Russian and Chinese, and a little bit of Spanish, Portuguese, and a few words in Mayan."

Boutros panted. "How can I help a beautiful young international lady like yourself?"

Lucas bowed his head in shame. This Boutros guy was in love . . . with his sister! Yuck.

"We were just thinking," said Astrid, "just hoping someone at the Good Company could tell us where Ms. Günerro's office is."

"Ah, Madame Günerro." Boutros rolled his eyes. "She changes offices like most people change underwear." He chuckled at his joke. "Excuse me. That was unprofessional." He straightened up quickly, and his expression and tone became almost robotic. "Madame Günerro is wonderful to us all. I would do anything to help her. But I don't know where her office is."

Hervé leaned over to say something to Lucas and Jackknife, but Astrid started talking.

"Boutros," she whispered. "You would do *anything* for Ms. Günerro?"

"Of course."

"Would you do *anything* for me?"

"If Madame Günerro would like it."

"Ms. Günerro would like for you to give me a key," Astrid said with a twinkle in her eyes.

Boutros was butter again. "I'll be honest with you," he said as he stared into Astrid's eyes. "I've worked for the Good Company since I was five," he said. "I'm eleven months away from seventeen, and I have aspirations of great success within the Good Company."

During this conversation several new guests had arrived and were waiting in an ever-growing reservation line. Two more clerks came out and began checking in other guests. Boutros briefly peeked over Astrid's head to see the end of the line. Lucas slithered his hand around Astrid's back, snatched the Globe Hotel key card back, and shoved it into his sock.

Astrid moved to close her argument. "I need a master key card, Boutros. Now."

More robot than human, Boutros Svengalvik inserted a Good Hotel card into a silver reader and punched a series of numbers into the keypad. "Without my manager's approval, I can only add one hour of time to the card. After that it must be reset. I hope that will be good enough for you, Miss . . . ?"

"Benes," said Astrid.

"Ah." Boutros nodded. "A good name."

Astrid blew him a kiss and snatched the master key card. "You're a doll."

"Here, it's my gift to you," said Boutros as he also gave Astrid a Navigo card. "The PIN is 7777."

She took the card, glanced at it, and slid it into her back pocket. Then she and the three boys walked away.

"Boutros is one messed-up dude," said Jackknife. "Like brainwashed."

"What?" Astrid said. "He liked me."

"Boutros is brainwashed, yes," said Hervé. "No one has 'aspirations of great success' within the Good Company. It's part of his brainwashing. But he, like me and others, is only half-brainwashed, because they used the old method."

Lucas said. "What does *that* mean?"

"How do I explain?" said Hervé, talking to himself. "You know that the Good Company brainwashes all new Curukians in a special ceremony. This you know. Right?"

They all nodded.

"The ceremony is only the beginning. There are many levels of brainwashing, and consequently there are . . ." Hervé bit his lip. "There are also secret ways to undo the brainwashing."

Jackknife asked the obvious question. "How?"

They stopped at the bank of elevators, and Astrid hit the UP button.

"You see . . ." Hervé paused. "I know Boutros. He and I both are working with a doctor to undo our brainwashing. But Boutros is not having much success. We *were* part of the Good Company. We were kidnapped together in the same year."

"Oh," said Astrid. "That's awful."

"I knew it," said Lucas. "You *are* part of the Good Company."

"I *was*," said Hervé defensively. He looked ashamed and sad and angry at the same time. "I am in the middle of undoing my brainwashing. It can take more than a year to free yourself from Madame Günerro's grip. But Boutros keeps going back to work for Madame Günerro. Why, I don't know."

Astrid nodded knowingly. "Sounds kind of like Stockholm syndrome, where hostages actually start to like their captors."

"Exactly!" Jackknife said. "That's exactly what Travis called it."

"But now," Hervé explained, "the Good Company methods are unbreakable. Unless caught early, it is very difficult to stop a brainwashing."

Jackknife pressed for the answer. "So how do you undo this brainwashing?"

"For some there are sounds," Hervé explained, "certain sounds that uh . . ."

"Stop right there!" A loud voice thundered down the hallway. "Hervé Piveyfinaus, stop."

The two security guards who had been in the lobby café came charging at the group. They were an odd-looking pair. One was heavy with clothes too small. The other was scrawny with clothes too big. They looked even more ridiculous with powdered sugar from the beignets still on their faces and jackets.

Hervé looked frightened. "I cannot return to the Curukians," he pleaded.

The elevator dinged and the door opened.

Lucas could tell that Hervé wasn't lying. "Run."

Jackknife said, "He can't run with a cane."

"We'll block them for you," said Lucas.

"Be careful," said Hervé as he hobbled down the hallway. "There are hidden passages in this hotel."

"Meet us at the safe house," Astrid called out.

"Where is it?" Hervé called back faintly.

Lucas, Jackknife, and Astrid couldn't answer. They were too busy bumping into the security guards and slowing them down. By the time the guards broke free, Hervé was long gone.

"Let's find Gini first," said Lucas.

Jackknife shrugged. "And Hervé, too, I guess."

"We've got a master key to the whole hotel," said Lucas. "Let's search every room."

ROOM SERVICE

Lucas, Astrid, and Jackknife stepped off the elevator on the second floor and stood looking dumbly at a sign that said first floor. Lucas remembered that in Europe they called the second floor the first.

Whatever, he thought. *It's different.*

Jackknife wandered down the hall by himself toward an abandoned cleaning cart.

Astrid sighed. "So this is your brilliant plan," she said, flashing the master key card. "Check every room? Have you done the math?"

"Uh . . ." said Lucas. "As a matter of fact, I have. I just need to multiply . . ." Lucas ran the numbers. "There were seventeen windows on the north side of the building, so seventeen times four sides times eleven stories equals seven hundred forty-eight rooms. Max. Some of these windows would be storage closets."

Astrid did her own math. "You expect us to search seven hundred forty-eight rooms in one hour?"

"Divided by sixty minutes," said Lucas, calculating, "that's about twelve rooms per minute."

"Impossible," said Jackknife as he came back, pushing the cleaning cart down the hall.

"Five seconds per room," said Lucas, sounding confident. "Open a door. Look in. Move on."

Jackknife opened a bin on the cleaning cart and found snacks for the minibar. He poured an entire bag of dark chocolate almonds into his mouth.

He muttered, "Lookatallthisstuff."

Astrid shook her head. "I still think we should go to the safe house."

"We will," said Lucas. "In an hour. As soon as we check the rooms."

Astrid's face was blank. "Somebody's going to call the managers and tell them there's a group of kids opening all the doors."

Lucas knew she was right. He saw how stupid Jackknife looked eating all that food at once. And he was stealing from a cleaning cart. Lucas figured that at this rate Jackknife might end up stealing sheets and towels.

Lucas snatched the master key card from his sister. "We'll start here," he said, putting the key card into the lock.

"That's a cleaning closet," said Astrid. "You're wasting time."

Lucas opened the door anyway. "That's it," he said excitedly. He pulled three housekeeper uniforms from a shelf. "Here," he said. "Put these on over your clothes."

"You've got to be kidding," said Astrid. "I am *not* wearing that."

"Yaw," mumbled Jackknife with a full packet of crackers in his mouth. "That's schupid."

Lucas had already slipped his room-service outfit over his clothes. It was a blue-and-white pinstripe tunic with double-breasted buttons. It would look terrible on anyone, but on Lucas it looked terrible and ridiculous.

"We have no choice," he said. He knocked on a door. "Service," he called out with a French accent. Then he opened the door with the master key and looked into the hotel room. There was no one.

Lucas tossed a uniform to Astrid and another to Jackknife. "One room down," he said. "Seven hundred forty-seven to go."

Dressed as housekeepers, they started opening doors to the hotel rooms, not knowing what they would find. "Service," they called out. The first few rooms had no people. In the fourth room a TV was on with no one watching. In the fifth room they heard somebody in the shower. Jackknife inserted the key card into the next door and opened it, only to find a plump and very hairy man in his underwear, yawning. Quickly Astrid pulled the door closed.

"Okay," she said. "This is not working. And this is gross. And kind of weird."

"This is not about what you don't want to see," said Lucas as he opened another door. Three little kids were jumping on the beds. No Gini. Lucas closed the door without the kids even noticing. "This is about finding the people we're missing."

The three teenage housekeepers kept moving down the hallway. They checked every room and moved to the next floor.

Lucas started pushing the cleaning cart. He smirked at Jackknife. "That outfit looks great on you."

"Thanks," said Jackknife. "That blue pinstripe really accents your eyes."

"Why thank you," Lucas said.

Astrid rolled her eyes and grabbed the master key card.

Halfway through this floor they fell into a rhythm of Astrid inserting the key card, Jackknife actually opening the door (Astrid not looking in), and Lucas scanning the room for clues and familiar people. At the top of Lucas's list were Gini, his dad, and any other New Resistance member, including Hervé Piveyfinaus.

"What's the deal with Hervé?" Lucas said. "Really."

"Leave him alone!" Astrid said.

"I'm sorry," said Lucas. "I don't know whether to believe him or not."

Jackknife stole another pack of crackers from the cart. "I'm not sure I trust him either."

"I mean," said Lucas, "he's helpful and all, but . . ."

"Maybe," said Astrid, "we don't understand what half-brainwashed is all about. Maybe he's just different."

Astrid held on to the key card and sped them along.

Lucas felt like every other door they opened seemed to have people who were either half-clothed or full-on naked. They continued with the fourth, fifth, and sixth floors. On the seventh floor their luck changed.

For the worse.

The seventh floor was freezing. Lucas knew they must be close, because Hervé had said Ms. Günerro liked to divert the air-conditioning to her office. Astrid curled her shoulders inside her uniform. Jackknife rifled through another condiment cart, lifted a bag of chips, and ate his way through the cold.

Lucas checked his internal clock. "This card's about to expire. There's not enough time."

"Told you," Astrid said through rattling teeth.

Jackknife shrugged. "What's your deal with that baby?"

"He made her a promise," said Astrid.

Lucas took the card back and jammed his hands in the uniform's front pockets. "I'll figure it out," he said. "They've got to be on this floor. Just start knocking on doors, and I'll open the ones on this side with the key card."

As it turned out, most rooms on the seventh floor of the Good Hotel were not really hotel rooms but more like double rooms that had been converted into little conference quarters. Astrid and Jackknife knocked on doors. She greeted the guests in French while Jackknife tried to speak French. He kept saying "wee, wee, wee," in an awful French accent, which

Lucas thought was a dead giveaway.

At room 722, Lucas noticed the shadow of a foot underneath the door, pacing back and forth. He could hear water running in pipes. A rush of adrenaline filled his veins. With the master key card, he opened the door.

In this room there was no artificial light, only faint sunlight shining through a curtain. Lucas tiptoed into the room and found a TV on but muted. On the bedside table a cigarette smoldered in a full ashtray, giving the whole room a dead smell. Somebody was whistling badly as the toilet flushed.

Then Lucas heard a baby cry.

Astrid crashed through the hallway door. "Now that was a baby!" she said. "Where'd it come from?"

Lucas pointed at the adjoining room. The toilet flushed again, and there was more whistling. Then water splashed in the sink.

With half a chocolate bar in his mouth, Jackknife peered into the room. "Um," he muttered. "Curukians in the hall."

From the adjoining room Gini let out a screeching squeal.

The bathroom door opened and knocked Lucas in the back. Lucas turned and slammed the door into the stunned Curukian's face as Jackknife side-kicked the boy in the gut. The Curukian stumbled backward, ripping the shower curtain from its rod. Jackknife looked at the kid lying in the bathtub and then shoved the second half of his chocolate bar into his mouth.

Lucas kicked open the privacy door between the two rooms.

Two Curukians were swinging Gini around the room, sweeping her feet against the lampshade. Lucas couldn't believe what he was seeing. The boy swinging Gini by the arms moved toward the window.

"Cut it out!" screamed Lucas.

When the boy tossed Gini on the bed, Jackknife sprang into action. Literally. He did a standing front flip, leaping over the bed. Three-quarters of the way through the flip, both his feet landed directly on the boy's chest. The Curukian never saw it coming. He fell backward and slumped against the wall.

While Jackknife was flying through the air, the other boy jumped on Lucas's back. The two of them were swinging around the hotel room until Lucas rammed him against the wall. In one fluid motion Lucas flipped the boy over his shoulders and flat onto his back. Astrid yanked the boy up and dragged him to a closet where she flung him on the carpet.

"Sorry," said Astrid as she slammed the closet door.

Lucas grabbed Gini from the bed and followed Astrid and Jackknife into the hallway only to find they were not alone. Five Curukians were waiting by the elevators.

"So, Mr. Mom," Astrid said to her brother, "now what are we supposed to do?"

Lucas didn't have a clue. "I'm working on it."

Astrid took the master key card from Lucas and tried it in the next door. It was dead. She pulled out the Navigo card she'd gotten from Boutros and tried it in the door. She handed Lucas the cards.

"What is this?" Lucas asked.

Jackknife looked at it. "That's a Navigo bike pass. It unlocks a city rental bike."

"We don't need a bike pass," said Astrid. "It doesn't work on the doors."

In the hallway, the Curukians still didn't move. They just stood outside the elevators, waiting.

The boys made Lucas rethink everything. He suddenly pictured himself handcuffed in a jail full of other failed New Resistance members, lost in some dark unknown prison in France. Then he remembered one of the housekeepers at the Globe Hotel telling him, "You can't save the world if you don't save yourself first."

Lucas knew he would have to do something totally unexpected. He reviewed his inventory. He had an unusable master key card, a Globe Hotel key card, a bike pass, a housekeeper's uniform, an eighteen-month-old baby, a sister, a friend, and five Curukians.

Not much to work with.

The elevator stopped, and Charles Magnus pulled open the lattice door. He and the two guards from the lobby café stepped into the hallway. Magnus was loosely holding Hervé in a half nelson. He and his two guards led Hervé down the hall as the Curukians followed in silence. Lucas, Gini, Astrid, and Jackknife were trapped. The two guards pushed them and shuffled them like prisoners to the end of the hallway.

The bigger guard zipped a chain from his pocket and inserted a key card into the door-handle reader. The reader beeped, its lights flashed green, and the door opened into a private office.

Lucas noted the room number: 777.

Triple sevens, he thought. *I am from Vegas. Could be lucky.*

THE LUCKY OFFICE

Luck was all they had left.

The Curukians stood guard in the hallway while Magnus and the two security officers led Astrid, Jackknife, Hervé, Lucas, and Gini into the room.

The hotel room had been converted into an interrogation cell—a rectangular room with only one door and no windows. From the ceiling a tin lamp dangled, casting a cone of white light on the table. The small silver box Lucas had seen in the airplane video was also on the table. Magnus took the device and attached it to the wall next to the light switch. The wall monitors immediately began clicking through live security-camera images of the streets of Paris.

Ms. Günerro sat at the opposite end of the table. In front of her, she had a mobile phone, a silver canister, and a bowl of frozen green peas. The poodle in pink panted at her side.

Lucas estimated their odds of getting out of the room safely at one hundred to one. They would need lots of luck and lots of skill. From his way of thinking, the only tool remaining was Astrid's obnoxious lawyerlike arguments. His sister didn't take long to load her words.

"Gosh," she started. "It's freezing in here!"

"Isn't it wonderful?" hissed Ms. Günerro. She pointed at a giant air-conditioning vent in the floor. "I had the technician divert all the cold air in the hotel to me."

"It's wasteful," sassed Astrid. "And disrespectful. Everyone else in the hotel is sweating."

For a second Ms. Günerro seemed a little surprised that somebody—a child—was challenging her. She quickly recovered.

"It's my hotel. I'll do what I want," said Ms. Günerro with a sinister chuckle. "Besides, Good guests will always pay extra for all things Good."

She sat up. "Now please, sit, and do tell me why you are paying me this wonderful visit."

The two guards snapped into action. The name tag on the tall, lanky teenager read GOPER BRADUS | NUUK, GREENLAND. There were specks of powdered sugar on his thin blond mustache. The other guard had roundish everything—glasses, cheeks, belly. His name tag read EKKI ELLWOODE EKKI | REYKJAVIK, ICELAND. Acting more like waiters than security officers, Goper and Ekki gracefully pulled out chairs for the children. As they sat, Gini wiggled free from Lucas and crawled along the table to Ms. Günerro's end. She stabbed both hands into the bowl of peas and began shoveling them into her mouth.

"I thought I got rid of this baby," said Ms. Günerro.

"I hate babies."

Astrid huffed. "You just told that group of reporters outside that you love babies."

"Young lady," said Ms. Günerro, glaring back. "What we say in public is not always what we mean in private. This is the way the grown-up world works."

Forever the lawyer, Astrid fired away. "Is kidnapping the way the grown-up world works too?"

"If you're making reference to my charity work with children, then you are sorely mistaken. So many children would lead miserably boring lives if it weren't for me and my Good Companies."

While Ms. Günerro and Astrid argued, Magnus stood behind Hervé and flipped through photographs in a white binder. He stopped at a picture and showed it to everyone at the table.

"Hervé Piveyfinaus," said Magnus, shaking his head. "This is an old picture of you, but I knew I recognized you. Look at you now, helping the Globe Hotel, or are you actually with the New Resistance?"

"Don't bother," said Ms. Günerro. "Half-washed kids always come and go. Hervé will do what I say when I need him the most. I will always own him."

Magnus eyed Jackknife. "And you're Paulo Cabral," he said. "AKA Jackknife."

"Yeah," Jackknife smirked.

"Had you on file for years," said Magnus.

Jackknife was sarcastic. "It's a pleasure to meet you in person."

"Here's your old mug shot." Like a dad showing pictures, Magnus held up a photograph of Jackknife drinking from a sippy cup.

"Let's get an updated photo." Magnus aimed his phone at Jackknife. "Good," he said. "You're from what? Bolivia, right?"

"Brazil."

"Same thing," muttered Magnus.

Magnus slapped another plastic page in his binder and then stared at Lucas and Astrid. "And you two must be John Benes's kids?"

Ms. Günerro wiped what seemed to be green pea juice from her lips. "I thought they all died in that ferry accident with the mother."

"Yes. The kids and everyone on the boat died," said Magnus. "But the mother had left the daughter with John Benes in Las Vegas."

Ms. Günerro pointed a long fingernail at Astrid. "That must be you," she said. "Just like your mother . . . confrontational."

Astrid stood. "Don't talk about my mother that way."

"Oh . . . I knew Kate," said Ms. Günerro. "Very well."

"You knew my mother?"

Ms. Günerro smiled wryly. "Kate Benes worked for me. Smart and always doing the right thing. She was VP at both Good Books and the Good Hotel. Yes. VP—very picky," she said. "Regardless, I too lost a lot in that accident."

"What!" Jackknife's voice cut across the table. "Her mother died in that accident." Then he slightly bent the truth. "And all her adopted siblings. Everybody on that boat died."

"It was a tragedy." Ms. Günerro's face was cold. "But Kate, as always, was trying to do the right thing, and she stole some very important account information from me, and those numbers supposedly died with her."

The room went quiet. Lucas's brain ran through every number he had ever seen in his entire life.

"So then," said Magnus, slowly pushing Astrid back into her chair. "What are your names? Lucy and Asterix?"

"Lucas and Astrid," said Astrid. "Thank you very much."

Magnus snapped two quick photographs of Lucas and Astrid.

"So," said Magnus confidently, "Lucas must be the kid from the other marriage—the divorce John Benes had."

Lucas said nothing. John Benes had never been divorced, but Lucas wasn't about to help Magnus correct this wrong information. The less they knew about Lucas and where he'd come from the better.

"What's your name again?" Astrid said, defiantly. "Mr. Mango?"

Ms. Günerro peered over her cat-eye glasses and leaned in. Her breath smelled of Coca-Cola Light, strawberry bubblegum, and cigarettes.

"Either this baby has a gas problem," she said, "or this dog needs to go out." She threw the leash across the room to Ekki.

"Take this beast outside," she said, then boasted, "The paparazzi loved my entrance with the dog today, didn't they? But enough is enough. I'd throw the baby out too, but"—she pointed at Astrid—"Little Miss Do Right here would argue up a storm. Like mother, like daughter."

"Uh . . ." stammered Ekki, clipping the leash to the dog's collar. "Taking the dog out is new-guy work, isn't it?" Ekki then handed the dog leash to Goper. "Here," he said dumbly. "You take it, and watch out for the Paris Poopercycle cop. He'll give you a ticket if you don't pick up."

"The what?" said Goper.

Magnus quickly checked the wall monitors showing updated street views from Paris's security cameras. "Go with him," said Magnus. "And pick up some oranges."

Ekki's brow furrowed. "What for?"

Siba Günerro flipped her phone around and showed the screen with the text *Oranges*.

"Because," said Magnus, "Hervé let us know that the New Resistance code was 'oranges.' I'm sure there are plenty of other New Resistance sympathizers still roaming around Paris. We want to talk with them."

Ms. Günerro chuckled in a sardonic tone. "The

New Resistance code this time has been raised to Code Orange. How witty!" Then Ms. Günerro pointed at the two guards. "Get out! I have a very large order to fill tomorrow night."

Ekki, Goper, and the dressed-up poodle squirmed out of the room.

Lucas looked across the table at his sister, hoping she had more verbal ammunition that would change their situation. In hotel-school Astrid could ask so many questions that the teacher forgot about teaching.

Astrid pointed to the silver canister on the table. "That's dry ice, isn't it?"

"Freon." Ms. Günerro smiled. "The blood of air-conditioning."

"Freon's toxic," argued Astrid.

"It's good for you," said Ms. Günerro.

Astrid fired back. "It's bad for the ozone."

In his mind Lucas marked another win for Astrid.

"Who cares about the ozone?" said Ms. Günerro. "Global warming is a hoax."

"But," said Jackknife, "why would you ever carry Freon or dry ice around with you, anyway?"

"I adore the cold," said Ms. Günerro. "My father was from Norilsk, and he named Siberia after me. . . . Or was it the other way around?"

Magnus coughed.

"Mr. Magnus here," said Ms. Günerro, "thinks you may have information about the Eiffel Tower?"

Astrid eyed Lucas and Jackknife. Lucas knew the

look. All they had to do was follow Astrid's lead and treat this woman as a substitute teacher and bombard her with ridiculous comments and questions.

Death by Middle School.

"The Eiffel Tower?" Astrid said smartly. "We know a lot."

"Well," Ms. Günerro coughed. "Do tell."

Astrid started. "The Eiffel Tower was built in 1889."

"Made of iron," said Jackknife. "It weighs ten thousand one hundred metric tons."

Lucas guessed: "More than two million rivets."

"Ribbit," said Jackknife, making a frog sound.

"One thousand six hundred sixty-five steps," said Lucas.

"That's enough!" Ms. Günerro spat. "I'm talking about security."

While Lucas, Jackknife, and Astrid were bombarding Ms. Günerro, Hervé was actually laughing.

Lucas saw the lawyer in Astrid light up again. "Wait a minute. You lost the security contract to guard the tower," she said, "so you had your Curukian boys kill those tourists, didn't you? You mugged and killed tourists so the new security company would look bad—really bad—and you'd get your contract back."

Gini slapped her little hands on the table. "Baaad," she mimicked. Then she stuffed more green peas in her mouth.

"I saw a sign about that carnival," said Jackknife. "You mugged and killed tourists at the Eiffel Tower days before your carnival? That doesn't make sense."

"Busball," Gini said.

"That's enough," snorted Ms. Günerro. "Tell that little boy to be quiet."

"She's a girl," Lucas, Astrid, and Jackknife said together.

"Girl," Gini echoed.

Astrid and Ms. Günerro were now locked in a death stare. Ms. Günerro snatched the bowl of peas from Gini.

"Pea," said Gini. "Pee-pee."

Lucas kept quiet and watched. Hervé snickered, and Jackknife picked up the pestering where Astrid had left off. He reached across the table and drummed his fingers on Ms. Günerro's mobile phone.

"Hey, Madame Günerro," said Jackknife. "If you're going to keep us here all day . . . can I play games on your phone?"

"Don't touch my phone," she said, slapping the phone back under her hand. "Magnus, get me some Curukian boys down here. Now."

Astrid didn't miss the chance. "There's no such thing as Curukians."

"They're from Raffish, Curuk," said Magnus.

Lucas said, "We all know geography."

"Yeah." Jackknife jumped in. "There is no Raffish, Curuk."

Gini burped. "Curuk."

Ms. Günerro had had enough. "You argumentative

little ninnies!" she cried. "You all should have your mouths washed, and brains washed too."

It was clear that the world leader in child labor didn't like spending that much time with children. Ms. Günerro slammed the dry ice canister on the table, sprang from the chair, and whacked her head on the hanging lampshade.

"Aahh," spat Ms. Günerro as she pushed Charles Magnus. They stormed out of the room, leaving the five children alone. The electronic locks bolted the door with a series of metal clangs.

Hervé, Jackknife, Astrid, and Lucas sat in the sterile office and listened to Ms. Günerro's hysterical arguments outside the locked door. Like a little Buddha, Gini sat on the table with the bowl of peas now between her legs.

Questions swirled in Lucas's mind. Apparently everyone else had unanswered problems too.

"Hervé?" Astrid asked. "So you really used to be a part of the Good Company?"

"Correct. I was . . . in the past," he said defensively. "My father was head of the chemical division in China, and of course as a child I worked all the time alongside him. I was one of the first to be tested with brainwashing drugs. Some worked. Others made me bald. But then I burned myself on the leg in a chemistry lab with a new substance on which my father was working, and it is why I cannot run correctly now."

Lucas furrowed his brow. "I thought you said you

had bone marrow cancer?"

"I lied," said Hervé. "I am sorry. If I had told you the truth in the beginning, you would never believe me now."

In an odd way Hervé seemed to make sense. But trying to put true and false information in the right categories was exhausting.

"I am on your side. Honest," Hervé pleaded with a shrug. "And I have access that no one else has."

"Lucas," said Astrid. "In the beginning, you were right about Hervé not telling the whole truth. But I think right now he's giving us a lot of information."

Lucas began to soften. He knew he had been right, and wrong. At least partly. He nodded at Hervé and Astrid.

"So, Hervé," Astrid continued. "Why does Ms. Günerro have the same room number that we have in Las Vegas?"

"Numbers mean different things to different people," said Hervé. "Madame Günerro may be using seven-seven-seven for a symbol of trust, while in Las Vegas you probably use seven-seven-seven as a symbol of luck."

"But luck," said Jackknife, "can be good or bad."

"It depends on how you choose to see things," said Hervé.

"Next," said Astrid, keeping up the barrage of questions, "what is Raffish, Curuk? It's not really a place. Or is it?"

"But of course," said Hervé. "Raffish, Curuk, is and is not a place. It is a—how would I say?—an anagramation of different places."

"You either mean," said Astrid, clarifying, "an anagram or an amalgamation."

"Maybe yes, maybe no," Hervé explained. "It is a Good Company name. It is an anagramation of US, UK, CHI, RF, FRA—the initials of all the members of the United Nations Security Council. The US, the UK, China, Russia, and France."

"What?" Lucas said. "I thought the UN was supposed to be good. The Good Company is not."

"Again," said Hervé, "it depends on how you choose to see things."

Astrid rolled her eyes. "Kerala's right. Everything's upside down with this company. I can't deal with this."

Jackknife nodded. "If the Good Company controls the UN, then they could do whatever they want and have the backing of the world. Every country would support what the Good was doing."

Outside the door Ms. Günerro was chewing someone out. The kids glanced toward the noise.

Astrid declared, "We should go to the safe house."

"Where is that?" Hervé sprang back to life. "I am looking for it all of the times."

Lucas knew Hervé was helping them a lot, but the French kid was maybe just a little too excited. Half-washed brain could mean half helping the New Resistance, half helping the Good Company. Lucas was in no hurry to make a mistake.

"It's the, um . . ." Lucas paused, trying to think of the opposite of the Shakespeare and Company bookshop. "It's at the Café l'Abri, just across the street from the hotel."

Jackknife added to the white lie. "Yeah," he said. "We chose that spot because it was so close to the Good Hotel."

The look on Hervé's face was puzzled. "Very strange indeed," he said. "But . . . but . . . okay. Things are always in reverse with the Good Company."

Lucas was interested. "Why do you say that?"

Hervé paused. "The Café l'Abri is where Madame Günerro likes to take refuge. She owns the place and often takes her business there."

"What do you mean, 'business'?" Jackknife asked.

"It suffices to say," said Hervé, "that you don't want to do business with Madame Günerro at the Café l'Abri. It is the beginning of the end for you."

Astrid turned the question back on Hervé. "So then the Café l'Abri is a hideout," she said. "Is there some sort of safe house for the Good Company?"

"In Paris, the Curukians have many secure houses," Hervé explained. "There is Bois de Boulogne, Saint-Denis, and an apartment building near the Sacred Heart, where the Brainwashing Ceremony begins."

Lucas memorized the places and then asked, "How do you know which apartment building it is?"

"That group loves fire," Hervé said. "Look for a burned car. But at the Sacred Heart safe house you also have to watch out for *le . . . le . . .*"

Suddenly the door opened, and Ms. Günerro and Magnus barged back into the room, silencing them all.

CURUKIAN PROPOSAL

Ms. Günerro entered the cold room, acting as if nothing had just happened. She calmly slid her chair out and sat at the table. Over the top of her cat-eye glasses she glared at the children in front of her. She tossed a few frozen peas in her mouth and inhaled white fog from the silver canister. The Freon, or dry ice, or whatever it was seemed to calm her down.

"I'd like to make you all an offer," Ms. Günerro said evenly. She leaned on the table and paused. "I've come to the conclusion that I could well use your services."

No one said anything.

Ms. Günerro spoke in a kind voice. "We've been looking for some smart children like you to help us recruit other children to a better life—to a Good life."

Magnus pointed at the monitors. "We've been watching you. And we think you all are very good."

Astrid argued. "You can't just watch people—that's creepy."

"Paris is the most visited city in the world," Magnus explained. "There are a lot of tourists to keep safe. That is why the Good Company is paid to serve and protect."

"Which is why we need more people to work with us." Ms. Günerro's eyes rose across the table. "Which brings me back to my proposition for you four."

Astrid spoke first. "I don't want to have anything to do with you."

"No thank you," said Jackknife. "But could you pass the peas please? I'm starved."

"Peas," said Gini.

"I've already worked for you," said Hervé. "And I lost my hair and part of my leg."

"Hervé," said Ms. Günerro. "Once a Good boy, always a Good boy. I will always control you."

There was silence for a second as the cruelty of her words sank in.

"And," Ms. Günerro said, "you haven't even heard my offer." She smiled. "I have a gentleman in Africa who would pay you handsomely—millions each."

"Bunguu?" Jackknife asked.

Ms. Günerro seemed shocked. "How do you know Mr. Bunguu?"

"We've done our homework," said Astrid.

Ms. Günerro smiled. "Precisely why Mr. Bunguu and I would like to hire smart children like you."

The CEO swung her eyes around the table and stopped at Lucas.

"And you, young man?" she said, slicing the silence. "You've yet to speak."

Lucas scratched the back of his neck and considered the possibilities. He knew Astrid's method of pestering was good for winning arguments, but ultimately her technique would never work against a person as ridiculous as Ms. Günerro. If Lucas was ever going to find out about his mothers, then he would need to know how Siba Günerro thought and how she worked.

He smiled. "I'd like to hear more about your proposal."

"I'm glad you've come to your senses," said Ms. Günerro. "You see, part of the Good Company's mission is to save children around the world."

"That's full-on child labor you're talking about!" Astrid fired back.

"I'll let Lucas decide," said Ms. Günerro in a disturbingly calm voice. "Since you all have already refused an offer you haven't even heard."

"Go ahead," said Jackknife.

Ms. Günerro grinned. "Here's what I would like to offer you," she said. "You can choose to work with me on my management team and keep your mind just the way it is now. Simple. If you choose this option, you will come and live and work with me and the Good Company. I will house you in the very best Good Hotels throughout the world. You will be waited on like a king. You will be allowed to sleep late every day. And there will be no school and no homework."

Lucas mulled the idea. Everything Ms. Günerro did was way over the top. The Good Hotels were nicer than the Globe Hotels. Everybody knew that. And no school was something Lucas had always dreamed of.

"Or option two," Ms. Günerro continued. "I can take you all to a ceremony, and you will become like good Curukians and you'll do as I say. Forever."

Astrid huffed. "Same thing either way. We end up working for you."

"You've already refused the proposal," Ms. Günerro said, pointing at Astrid, Jackknife, and Hervé. "You all have chosen option two by default."

Lucas raised his eyebrows and knotted an idea in his brain.

"Lucas?" Ms. Günerro's eyes burned a hole in him.

Lucas delayed her game as he put the finishing touches on the idea. He could tell that Astrid and Jackknife and Hervé were all getting a little nervous with his slow response. But Ms. Günerro seemed to hate Lucas's silence the most.

"I have an idea," said Ms. Günerro. "We could brainwash you one at a time." She pointed at Gini. "Whom should we brainwash first, Lucas? The baby? Or has that been done?" She pointed at Jackknife. "Your friend?" She nodded toward Hervé. "The Frenchman?" Then she pointed at Astrid. "Or your sister?"

Lucas calculated. Everything was backward with the Good Company. Ms. Günerro ran the most powerful behind-the-scenes company in the world. She must be smart, somehow, Lucas reasoned. He knew that he, too, had to act differently. It dawned on him that the best way of dealing with somebody like Siba

Günerro would be the opposite of normal. Things would never be good with the Good Company unless he did something about it—in a way that no one else had ever done before. This was his father's plan all along. The only way Ms. Günerro could run things was by creating total confusion among those around her. It was a fantastically unintelligent way to operate a company, but no one could beat her because no one really understood the rules of her games. Like it or not, Lucas had to change tactics.

"I'll make you a deal," said Lucas, pulling the baby to his lap like a big brother. "Of course I'd like to help everyone, but obviously that's not possible. If you let the others go and I get to keep this baby, then I will work for you and your management team."

Lucas turned to look at Astrid, hoping she would trust him. The look on her face was pure and total confusion. She looked at Hervé and Jackknife.

"Help me out here, guys," she pleaded.

Before either boy could speak, Lucas stole the show again. "I don't want them either," he said, turning to Ms. Günerro.

"I wasn't born yesterday, young man," said Ms. Günerro. "That's exactly what you do *not* want me to do." With a sinister grin, she nodded knowingly. "But your scam is also a trap, because you want me to take them and leave you here with the baby? Right? I'm no fool. You're trying to trick me into thinking that you're trying to trick me, when in reality you're trying to trick me into thinking that you're not tricking me."

"How did you ever guess?" Lucas said. "I mean how did you ever know that that was exactly what I don't want you to do, so you would do exactly not the opposite of what you think is a trick that is not actually a trick at all?"

Ms. Günerro looked at Magnus. "We'll do the exact opposite of what Mr. Lucas Benes has said not to do. Is that clear?"

Magnus looked clueless. He opened the door, stuck his foot on the threshold to block the door open, and signaled to his Curukians in the hallway. The six boys stank of stale cigarettes as they entered the room. They grabbed Astrid, Hervé, and Jackknife by the arms and escorted them from the room, leaving Lucas and Gini behind.

Ms. Günerro joined Magnus at the door. He handed her a master key card, which she slipped into the small silver box on the wall. A light on the card reader flashed green. The monitors went black for a second, and then a video began to play. The screens started with a numbered countdown from ten.

"Say good-bye to your past," said Ms. Günerro. "And prepare to embrace the Good you have within." She turned off the room light. "After you and your little friend watch this video, I will return and we will begin again."

Calmly, Ms. Günerro and Magnus glided out of the room. The door closed behind them, and the electronic security device locked.

The video countdown was at six.

Lucas put Gini on the table with the bowl of peas. Immediately he went to the reader on the wall and removed Ms. Günerro's master key card. Nothing happened.

The video countdown was at four.

Lucas flung Ms. Günerro's master key card to Gini on the table and then tried the Navigo bike pass. He jammed it into the slot. Dead. Then he remembered the Globe Hotel key card in his sock. It didn't work either.

The video countdown was at two.

Lucas started to snap the cards in his hand, but Gini began to crawl off the table at the same time. Without thinking, Lucas pivoted and grabbed her before she fell.

The brainwashing video opened with a faded picture of Siba Günerro.

"I'm sorry, Gini," he said.

On the video, Ms. Günerro's hypnotic face was slowly coming into focus.

Holding Gini to his chest, Lucas leaned against the door in defeat. His eyes were strangely drawn to the movie. Part of him was itching to know what she was doing in that video to brainwash kids. Gini grabbed the plastic cards from Lucas and started chewing on them. Then she leaned toward the wall and stuck the expired master key card—the one they had with them to open all the hotel doors—into the reader. As her little thumb hit the microchip in the card, a light flashed green on the card reader.

The video stopped abruptly and the screens went black.

When Lucas touched his thumb on the key card in the reader, a red light flashed and the machine spit the card out.

"You reset it!" Lucas said. "With *your* thumb."

Lucas pocketed the cards.

From the hallway they heard a raspy voice.

"I forgot my Freon!" shrieked Ms. Günerro from the other side of the locked door. She slapped the door handle like a four-year-old in a tantrum. "And this stupid door is electronically locked! I hate locks!"

Lucas truly kicked in and went into a blur of motion in the darkness. He set Gini on the floor, pulled the housekeeper's uniform off, and threw it down. Then he felt around for the air-conditioning cover. He wrenched the metal grate off the vent and slid half his body down into the duct.

Ms. Günerro beat on the door. "I forgot my Freon!"

Gini shivered. "Wala."

"I'm not leaving you," said Lucas as he balanced his body inside the duct. Then he grabbed Gini, wrapped her arms around his neck, hugged her tight, and started to shimmy down into the air-conditioning duct.

Gini mumbled into Lucas's neck. "Frefrah," she said.

"I was thinking the same thing," said Lucas as he lifted himself up from the floor vent. He slapped around on the table until he found the bottle of dry ice. He cranked open the valve on the canister to full, and the room began to fill with fog.

Gini stuck her tongue out and said, "Pppppppp."

Lucas positioned himself inside the air-conditioning duct and replaced the metal grate on the floor above him. Then he and Gini descended into the hidden passages that Hervé had told them about.

DUCK IN THE DUCT

Peering through the air-conditioning vent above his head, Lucas saw the light to the Lucky Office switched on. Ms. Günerro, Magnus, and a Curukian boy stepped into the dry-ice fog. Lucas could hear them frantically moving the table and chairs in the near-blinding haze.

Ms. Günerro shrieked. "I can't see!"

"It's your ridiculous Freon," barked Magnus. "We can't see anything in this smog."

"The baby," said a Curukian boy. "It's gone."

Another Curukian said, "And they stopped the video."

"Impossible," Magnus said.

"Get the baby," Ms. Günerro stated, "and you'll get them both."

Lucas could hear Magnus's walkie-talkie squawking as he and Gini inched down the duct.

"Wala," Gini cried, her tiny voice echoing in the duct.

"Sorry," said Lucas, who was squishing his legs against the sides of the duct for support. "I can't see, you know. We are in a duct."

"Duck," Gini repeated.

A few minutes later Lucas and Gini came to an intersection. The metal tubes seemed to be converging and dropping down into a cooling unit. The blowing air soon became fierce and cold. Gini's thin wispy hair was whipping straight into Lucas's face, tickling his nose. Lucas tried to squeeze through the largest chute. When his shoe rattled against a fan blade, he knew he'd gone the wrong way. From the opposite side of this intersection, he saw a light. Then a voice called out.

"Give me your foot."

"Dad?" Lucas answered. "Dad?"

"Yeah."

His dad's voice sounded muffled with all the noise from the air-conditioning. He and Gini scooted deeper into the duct and closer to his dad.

"Move back," Lucas called out. Then he kicked the metal grate, and the vent flew off and clattered on the floor. Lucas put his face down and tried to peer into a garage.

"Hello," he called out. "Dad?"

"Hand me the baby first."

With his elbows and knees wedged against the metal walls, Lucas slowly peeled Gini's arms off his neck. Then, holding her by her arms, he dangled her down through the vent.

"Got her."

Lucas's dad didn't sound right to Lucas. He looked through the vent again and smelled gasoline. Lucas sucked in and corkscrewed himself down through the opening. He hopped down and into the garage, where the slap of his shoes echoed across the concrete floor.

He couldn't believe what he saw. He couldn't believe what he had just done. He had wanted his dad to be there so badly that he had made himself believe it was his dad's voice.

There was Gini, strapped with a series of bungee cords to the back of Goper's motorcycle.

Ekki and Goper started their two Ducati motorcycles, and the sound blasted through the garage, echoing off the cement walls.

The Ducatis were both Hypermotard 1100 EVO SPs. The engines, at 7,500 revolutions per minute, had the ability to reach the equivalent of ninety-five horses at full speed. Lucas knew that if the motorcycles left the garage, he would most likely never see Gini again.

The two Ducatis eased up the ramp, the engines grumbling for action. Gini swatted Goper's curly hair from her face. Then the racing bikes peeled out and into the streets of Paris, leaving Lucas alone in the dead silence of the garage.

GREEN IS GOOD

Things at the Good Hotel were never as they seemed.

Sometime in the middle of the afternoon, Lucas Benes stepped out the back door of the hotel and stood alone at the edge of the Parisian sidewalk, scanning the street, seeing nothing familiar. The fourteen-year-old held tears back as he focused on his failures. He had lost everyone—his father, his sister, his best friend, and two mothers. Now he had lost Gini, the one person he had promised to keep. He had lost her twice.

Lucas felt awful. He began to believe what everybody always said about him. He was just a mediocre kid who couldn't do anything very well. Neither good nor bad. He was nothing. The only thing Lucas knew that could make himself feel better was to catalog everything he saw.

In one snapshot section of the city block in front of him there were: ninety-seven cars, twenty-two parked along the curb, and six red ones; three police officers, two on horseback; and nine Curukian boys in three separate clumps. There were six trash cans, one postal box, five cafés, one Vélib' bike-rental station with fifteen out of eighteen bikes, two banks, fourteen apartment buildings, and one security camera mounted on a light pole, scanning. There were four crosswalks and seventeen directional signs on the street, three of which had the red "no entry" symbol. Directly across the street the Café l'Abri, with its red awning, was half-full with tourists and locals. Sitting in one of the cane-back chairs on the sidewalk was Hervé. Just behind him in the shadow three Curukian boys waited. Lucas memorized it all.

Lucas felt a little better. In his mind he jotted a list of the things he needed to do:

Save Gini.
Save Astrid.
Find out about Dad.
Get to the Shakespeare and Company safe house.
Get to a Curukian safe house?
Save Jackknife.
Save Hervé?
Save yourself, first.

Standing alone on the sidewalk, Lucas reflected on the last item on his list. Thoughts swirled in his brain. *You can't save anyone if you don't save yourself. And forget about everybody else—they always forget about me. And scratch Hervé—I don't know what he's doing.*

"Yeah," he muttered aloud to himself. "Forget everybody else."

The sound of his own voice startled him and brought him back to reality. He checked around to see if anyone had heard him talking to himself. Still very much alone, Lucas began walking behind two random men in business suits who had just come from a bar. He moved to blend in with a group of women so he could check out the Vélib' bike-rental station.

Lucas pulled out the Navigo pass that Boutros had given Astrid in the hotel. No sooner had he fallen in love with the idea of a bike than he figured this bike card could be a trick too. But it occurred to him that the bike card was all that he had at this point. He set the card on the reader and entered the PIN that he heard Boutros give to Astrid. Then Lucas chose bike number fourteen because it was his fourteenth birthday. The bike unlocked itself from the rack.

"Happy birthday, Lucas," he said to himself.

The brand-new bike had a retro design with fenders, a basket on the handlebars, and a cushy black seat. Lucas straddled the bike and scooted between two parked cars, where he peeked through the car windows. From this new angle Lucas could see a dress shop, a veterinarian shop, a jewelry store, and twenty-two pigeons.

The same two motorcycles that Lucas had just seen leaving the garage returned. The two Ducatis rolled down the middle of the street and skidded to a stop in front of the Café l'Abri. Gini seemed to be sleeping in the bungee-cord bundle, her head cocked to the side.

From his vantage point Lucas could see well into the open-air café. A line of waiters seemed to be standing guard on the sidewalk, and at a corner table surrounded by Curukian boys were Astrid and Jackknife. Hervé was still sitting solo at a table on the sidewalk, sipping on a fizzy drink. Just under the awning of the café, Ms. Günerro listened to Magnus as she texted on her phone. She whispered something to him, and within seconds he was on a motorcycle. He wrenched the throttle, amping up the RPMs, making the bike scream into the street. The brand-new Pirelli Diablo rear tire began to spin and smoke on the asphalt as Magnus released the brake and spun the bike at full speed. He popped a wheelie and rode on the back wheel down the middle of the street, aimed straight at Goper and Ekki. Then he carefully set the bike down between the other two motorcycles.

Through the car windows Lucas watched Magnus. The man's look was smug as he killed the engine on his motorcycle. He muttered something to both men, and then the head of Good Company Security looked around the street and raised his gloved hand in the air. Then he thumped the sleeping baby square on the top of the head.

Gini woke up—howling.

Lucas had never been madder in his life. It was clear to him that this show was to flush him out of hiding, but he wasn't going to take the bait. Magnus restarted his motorcycle and thundered down the street past Lucas, who was still crouching behind the parked car.

Ekki pulled Gini from the makeshift cocoon on the back of Goper's bike and held the tiny girl as her screams echoed off the buildings. Goper grabbed the baby and took her in his arms. Gini quieted down. Slowly her fat cheeks began to swell. Her face turned bright red like she was choking.

Lucas was about to freak.

Then Gini's face turned purple.

The pea-green poop exploded with such force that most people in the street stopped what they were doing and looked around for the origin of the sound. Goper leaned back on the motorcycle and tried to avoid the lava flow of diarrhea pouring from every opening on Gini's diaper. Green goo splashed on his shirt and pants. It splattered his face and sprayed his curly hair. The scene was such a colossal mess that Goper held Gini in the air as if he were offering her for sacrifice.

Opportunity.

Lucas's heart beat in his throat. This would be a skill that he had never practiced in any training: re-kidnapping a kidnapped kid who was dangling in midair between two security guards on motorcycles in the middle of a street in a foreign country. And the kid he had to re-kidnap was covered in green diarrhea.

There was a first time for everything.

Lucas scooted his bike around the parked car. Out of sheer habit he added the car's license plate to memory. Then he set his foot on a pedal and pointed his bike directly between Goper's and Ekki's motorcycles. A rush of adrenaline thrust through his veins as he pumped his bike down the middle of the street. Lucas stood on the pedals and swayed the bike left and right, trying desperately to squeeze any remaining speed from the tires. As he approached the two motorcycles, Goper was still unceremoniously holding the poop-covered kid in the air. Lucas let go of his handlebars, crouched, and kept pedaling.

In one motion he sat up straight, grabbed Gini under the arm, and snatched her away. Lucas's bike started to wobble as he pedaled faster toward the curb. Then he spun Gini in the air and plunked her down into the basket on the handlebars.

Within the next thirty seconds Lucas pedaled hard around the first corner, down an alley, and out of sight. In his mind he knew somewhere hidden in the city there were other Curukians preparing to capture him. The feeling was so strong that he could almost see it happening in front of him.

A CITY CRAWLING WITH CURUKIANS

In a Curukian safe house on the other side of Paris, a cell phone spun in a tight circle and vibrated on the wooden floor.

A tall, skinny East African boy flipped the phone open, scanned Ms. Günerro's text message, and then dialed her number. As the phone rang, he hit the light, which shed a dull yellow glow over the hostel's sleeping quarters. The space was jammed with twelve teenage Curukians, some half-asleep on bunk beds, all sweating profusely. The smell of armpits was so strong that roaches wouldn't even eat the crumbled baguettes scattered on the floor. In the corner three boys crowded around the bright light of a computer game.

"Yes, *madame*," said the tall boy into the telephone. His eyes looked like he had never smiled, ever. "It's just . . . we haven't done this before, so I wanted to verify the symbol on your text message. You're alerting all Curukian cells in Paris? All of them?"

He nodded confidently. "As you wish."

While still holding the phone to his ear, the tall

boy kicked the others away from the computer. He kneeled, clicked on his email, and looked at the picture of Lucas sitting in Ms. Günerro's Lucky Office.

"I have the photograph that Mr. Magnus sent," said the tall boy. "The boy's name is Lucas and he's rented a Vélib' bike. Is that correct?" He nodded as Ms. Günerro spoke. "Consider it done."

"Let's go," said the tall boy as he slapped the phone closed. He banged his knuckles on a sign on the door. The sign, faded and etched with a knife, read NEVER FORGET: RAFFISH, CURUK.

The other boys snapped to attention. Dressed in black, twelve apostles of Ms. Günerro rolled out of the room and marched down the stairs and into the streets of Montmartre.

The street was arguably the ugliest in Paris, with bombed-out cars, vacant buildings boarded up, and trash rotting everywhere. The line of sleepy Curuki-ans moved steadily outside, where the boys kicked dead pigeons into the street. The last boy in line, a lanky kid no older than Lucas, straggled behind. He fiddled with something in his hand and then scraped a lighter across his thigh to set a Molotov cocktail on fire. He looked at it, blew slightly, and let the fire engulf the cloth fuse. Then, backhanded, he tossed the burning gasoline bomb into a parked car.

As the boys headed to the metro station, the fire consumed the car.

The tall East African boy signaled to split. At the top of the metro station, half went down the stairs into the subway system, while the others piled into a boxy black Citroën car. They sped away in a smoky cloud.

STINK

Magnus's motorcycle engine screeched like a modern dragon, echoing off the buildings in the sunless alley. The sound shocked Lucas out of his stunned state of mind. He entered a minefield of self-doubt, and the voice in his head killed his last drops of confidence. Coach Creed's words came back to him: "You gotta think before you act, boy." Lucas argued with himself. "I thought I should help that baby." Then Astrid's voice clawed at his brain. "We'll never find out what happened to my mother or yours if you don't learn what you're supposed to do. . . ."

At a forty-five-degree angle Magnus sped straight down the middle of the alley. Looking like a kid who didn't know how to ride a bike, Lucas wobbled his rented bicycle onto the cobblestone street. Gini bobbled in the basket and giggled in her diarrhea diaper.

Lucas didn't even look as he crossed the street. Had he glanced up, he would have seen Coach Creed waving from the back of a taxi painted with an Orangina advertisement. The taxicab flew down the middle of the wide avenue and skidded sideways, tires howling in a cloud of rubber smoke. It nearly knocked Lucas from his bike and blocked the entrance to the alley.

Lucas looked back.

Magnus dropped the front tire of the Ducati on the taxi's hood and rode up over the windshield, across the roof, and down the trunk. Three Curukians tracked around a corner at full speed, their boots slapping the stones. Lucas and Gini hopped a curb and cut diagonally through the Buren columns, under an archway, and onto another café-filled plaza where clowns juggled bowling pins for an audience. As Lucas rounded the fountain in the center of the plaza, he noticed his chest tightening.

Lucas hadn't had sports-induced asthma since he was in first grade. Now it was back and he had to get over it. Fast. He gulped air as he struggled to catch his breath. Gini seemed to be making fun of him. He couldn't help but laugh. It was just what he needed—a poop-covered baby in a bike basket making faces at him. The small laugh broke the asthma's grip, and he coughed.

"Hold on," he said.

As Magnus rode the Ducati onto the plaza, Lucas shot out across the street and through the intersection. His heart pounded in his chest as he dodged cars and rounded buses, like a rat in a maze. He pedaled underneath a stone archway and into Napoleon's Courtyard at the most famous museum in the world.

The Louvre.

Lucas spun around three hundred sixty degrees. For a second he and Gini gawked at the Louvre. The massive palace-turned-museum, which covered an area of more than seventy-five football fields, surrounded them on three sides. It was the Big Daddy of all museums.

He hurriedly walked the bicycle past the glass pyramid to the center of the courtyard, where he mixed in with the crowd, unnoticed by anyone except the security cameras. Around him tourists were wading in the fountain pools. Some were eating baguette sandwiches and chocolate croissants, others checking their cameras and putting on sunscreen.

Sunlight refracted through the giant pyramid, and light scattered across the water fountains. Magnus, Goper, and Ekki parked their motorcycles in the street and moved to the north side of the pyramid. Lucas and Gini quietly squeezed around a construction barricade. From there Lucas had a clear shot out. There was no time to second-guess.

Lucas bumped the bike down the stone steps and across the street. He rode around the miniature Arc de Triomphe and weaved through a maze of pebble pathways and into the Tuileries Garden.

The park was full of sunlight. Lucas took it all in. Flower beds framed green lawns. Benches and statues lined the walkways. Tourists strolled down the paths and through the woods. Under the trees waiters clanged metal chairs in a café. Lucas could smell coffee and roses. It made him think of his dad having Sunday morning breakfast on the patio at the Globe Hotel. At the park's far end the Ferris wheel he'd seen earlier spun in a circle on the place de la Concorde. Right in front of him some kids were having a birthday party with balloons.

"Some birthday party I'm having," Lucas sulked. "This stinks."

"Stink." Gini copied him. She craned her little neck back to look at Lucas. "Stink, stink," she repeated.

"Your diaper stinks," said Lucas flatly. "And I know somebody's got to change it, but I don't know how to change a diaper on a kid who's got stinky poop all over like you do. And I don't even have a diaper. And man does it stink!"

"Stink!"

Lucas got a little frustrated with her. "I know. I know, Gini, it is stinky, but I have a few other things on my to-do list."

Gini aped Lucas again. "Know," she muttered. "Stink."

"No," Lucas growled. "Your stinky is already here, and it's green and all over you. And I'm the one who . . ." Lucas paused.

He actually felt good about the way things were going. He had gotten away from Ms. Günerro, had gotten Gini back, and had biked faster than racing motorcycles. For the first time, probably in his life,

Lucas felt like he was good at being Lucas.

"Stink," Gini repeated.

There was something in the way Gini had said "stink" that made Lucas worried—like she knew something. Lucas looked over his shoulder, even though he didn't have to. He could now hear behind him the groan of a motorcycle engine and the crunch of tires on the gravel pathway.

THE TOUR DE PARIS

Emergency mode kicked in, and more adrenaline poured into Lucas's veins. He squished Gini farther into the basket so that her diarrhea diaper hit the bottom and her bare feet stuck out the top like two bull horns. Lucas locked his elbows as his sweaty palms slid into position on the handlebars. He pedaled the Vélib' bike down the gravel pathway, past the carousel and the trampolines, and past a group of boys playing soccer.

"Ball," Gini gurgled.

"That's right," said Lucas. "It's called football here."

"Busball here."

"Whatever."

Through the rows of plane trees Lucas could see the guards on the other side of the park trailing him, waiting for the right moment. Was he the only one in the New Resistance who hadn't been kidnapped, captured, removed from the field? The calculations in his brain went crazy as he tried to remember what he was supposed to do and where he was supposed to go.

This was hide-and-seek at the adult level. Playing this grown-up game of kidnapping was more than

Lucas had wanted. He coached himself. The safe house, they had said. He had to get to the Shakespeare and Company bookshop. He needed to reset. Unfortunately, the map of Paris in his brain turned to spaghetti.

When Lucas and Gini came to the end of the long Tuileries Garden, Lucas recognized the very bench he'd seen in the video where Siba Günerro and Charles Magnus had planned more kidnappings.

"I don't care," he muttered to Gini. "I don't care about the Good Company. Right now I just want to get us out of here."

It was terrifying. He felt like everyone in the park was staring at him. At hotel-school he had a red belt in tae kwon do. Here in Paris he had a chicken belt. He was afraid of everything. The voice in his head told him to run. But every muscle in his body was frozen. If he did nothing, they would just grab him. Again. Gini puttered her fat lips at Lucas. He shook his head and did the only thing a fourteen-year-old could do in this case.

Pedal.

Lucas rocketed to the fence at the end of the park and started to exit at the busiest intersection in Paris. Cars were zipping around the place de la Concorde and down the famous Champs Élysées. He knew the American Embassy was nearby, but they wouldn't believe his story. He was sure of that. At the far end of the wide avenue there was the Arc de Triomphe, and in the distance he spotted the tip of the Eiffel Tower.

"I don't even care about the Eiffel Tower."

"No Busball," said Gini.

"No what?"

"No Busball."

"No bubbles?"

"Busball."

"Gum balls?" Lucas was aggravated. "You're not making any sense, Gini. It sounds like you're speaking French and Arabic and English all mixed up. Like Frabarabarish, which is not even a word."

Gini repeated, "Frabarabarish."

Behind him the motorcycles' engines grumbled. Lucas knew he couldn't outrun motorcycles. But he might be able to lose them and make his way to the safe house. He closed his eyes for a second, and this time a map of Paris filled his brain.

The wrought-iron gate squeaked as Lucas opened it. He lowered the rented bike down the stone steps and onto the sidewalk. To his right was the most famous Globe Hotel in Paris, disguised under another name. In front of the entrance five Curukians sat on mopeds. Lucas and his eighteen-month-old friend then shot out across the street and through the invisible beam of another security camera.

He rode diagonally across the place de la Concorde and headed toward the river. It seemed only natural. The motorcycles trailed him. He pedaled fast across the Alexandre III bridge and zipped past Les Invalides hospital. He tried to turn left at the Rodin Museum, but Goper rode next to him, blocking his escape.

With his curly hair flapping in the wind, Goper grinned across a row of parked cars. The security guard seemed to be mocking Lucas by pretending to race him. The green diarrhea on Goper's face and in his hair had dried and crackled and made him look even more ridiculous.

Lucas came to the Montparnasse Tower. He would have to outthink the guards if he ever stood a chance at truly shaking them. This late in the day and this far south in the city, the only safe place for Lucas was with Coach Creed's Senegalese friends.

Southeast corner of the train station, Lucas reminded himself.

Quickly Lucas calculated everything he saw that might be of value to him. On the next block a construction site looked most promising. There was a backhoe, a dump truck, and a crew of men in hard hats assembling scaffolding on the sidewalk. One of the workers, wearing a reflective yellow vest, was unloading metal pipes from a truck.

Lucas swerved in front of the motorcycles. He headed straight for a huge hole in the road. If his math was right, the timing would be perfect.

The man in the reflective yellow vest pulled the next pipe from the truck. As with the other poles, he swung the metal pipe out over the street. Lucas bent forward and held Gini down in the basket as they glided under the pipe. He turned around just in time to see the metal pole smack Goper square on the forehead. His motorcycle wobbled for a second, and then Goper clunked heavily into the hole. Magnus and Ekki hit the brakes just in time, their rear tires screeching.

Lucas turned the next corner and slipped between two parked cars. He popped his bike over the curb, up the stoop, and into a butcher shop. If the map in his head was right, Coach Creed's Senegalese friends' shop should be in the alley behind the store.

The French butcher shop was a bloody blur, with plucked ducks hanging in the window. Lucas remembered his manners and said *bonjour* to the butcher and to the ladies waiting in line. Within seconds he and Gini had bombed through the shop, out the back door, and into an alley.

There it was: a tiny African shop, Le Gris Gris. A man dressed in a long colorful robe opened the back door. Standing next to him was Coach Creed.

Lucas walked the bike from one shop to the other. The inside of the African store was lively, jammed with fruit and vegetables and fabrics, and all kinds of little toys and trinkets. The whole store smelled of chicken and lemon and onions, and Lucas's hunger kicked in. He parked the bike by the cash register and nearly collapsed.

Coach was shaking his head the whole time. "You sure do cover a lot of distance on that bike, boy," he said. "Security cameras can barely keep up with you."

Lucas looked up at Coach and said nothing. He couldn't breathe. Coach gave him a liter bottle of water, which Lucas drank, spilling it down the front of his shirt.

"Glad you figured out how to get here. And . . ." Coach Creed said, looking at Gini in the basket. "How in world did you get that baby?"

"Long story," Lucas said.

"We got ourselves a mess out there," said Coach. He shook his head again. "Maybe it wasn't the best idea to send just kids out alone."

Lucas panted. "What happened with the fire on the plane?"

"Everybody's fine," Coach said. "The plane's a little messed up, but your dad's got a crew working on it. He sent me out here to bring you and the others back."

"Where are the others?"

"Ms. Günerro took them all from the hotel to one of *their* safe houses," said Coach. "Apparently Ms. Günerro is looking for some highly educated kids just like New Resistance kids. Meaning you, your sister—every single one of you in Tier One."

"Yeah, I know," Lucas said, "but I'm not leaving them behind."

"I don't want you hurt, son," Coach said. "I'm pulling the plug on this whole mission right here and now."

"What?" Lucas said.

Coach Creed said something in Wolof to the

Senegalese man, and he nodded and then took Lucas's bike. The man's wife then came out from behind a curtain and looked at Lucas and Gini. She was a plump woman wearing a colorful dress.

"*Bébé,*" said the woman.

"*Bébé,*" Gini copied.

The woman said something to Coach in Wolof. She then picked Gini up and whisked the diarrhea-covered girl back behind the curtain and into a room.

"You're going to need to spend the night here," said Coach. "Tomorrow is officially B-Day."

"B-Day?" Lucas asked.

Coach nodded. "Brainwash Day."

Lucas said nothing.

"I'll be back in the morning, and we'll go straight to the airplane and figure out how to get the others back," Coach said. "Fatima and I have been friends for a long time. She'll take care of you tonight."

"But . . ." Lucas started to say.

"End of story," said Coach. "I'll be back in the morning—when it's safe for you to leave. Right now every Curukian in the city is looking for you."

Coach Creed peeled the curtain back and said something in Wolof to Fatima, and then he disappeared out the shop's back door and into the alley.

Typical, Lucas thought.

Lucas was starving anyway, and the smell of chicken and lemons and onions was driving him mad. Fatima slid the curtain to the side and signaled for Lucas to follow her. He focused on the small table, where a huge plate of rice was piled high with chicken and lemons and onions.

Poulet Yassa, Lucas thought. *Yum.* He said thank you, sat down, and ate the entire plate without even drinking a drop of water.

After dinner, Lucas sat on the daybed in the corner and looked at his room for the night. It was no fancy hotel. Whitewashed walls decorated with maps of Africa. A string of prayer flags encircled the molding. There was a bookshelf filled with amulets, bird feathers, voodoo dolls, and other odd charms.

Gris gris, Lucas thought. *Juju to ward off wicked spirits.* He needed all the help he could get. A digital clock on a side table showed twenty hours. Lucas thought that felt right, about the same as the internal clock in his head.

Eight at night—eleven in the morning back at the Globe Hotel.

That was Lucas's last thought of the longest day of the year. His birthday. The events of the day finally hit him and hit him hard. He fell asleep on the daybed and didn't move a muscle all night.

THE LAST BEST HIDING PLACE

Lucas Benes lay in the daybed in the back room of Le Gris Gris in Paris, dreaming about a past that he was starting to remember. If he could travel in his mind, he might travel in time and remember the details that could point him to whatever it was he was looking for. With his eyes closed, Lucas listened. He could hear people in the store, shopping and talking. The smell of fresh bread was somewhere close by. Outside, a mixture of city sounds—trucks and cars and cafés—crept into the shop every time the door opened. The cash register dinged, and Lucas opened his eyes, sat up in bed, and looked at the clock.

Almost nine o'clock.

He had slept thirteen hours. Straight!

Lucas got up and moved toward the bread smell. Someone had left him a plate of chocolate croissants and a jar of pineapple juice. Probably Fatima.

As he ate, his father's compliment on the airplane came back to him. "You're man enough to know when to break a rule to help somebody in need. And that takes courage."

If Lucas was ever going to stand up for what was right and stand up against what was wrong, now was the time. The Good Company had killed his mothers. And now his sister and friends had been kidnapped and possibly could be getting brainwashed.

He felt overwhelmed by the choices he had to make. But was he, Lucas Benes, going to go back and sit on an airplane? With Coach Creed? And wait and hope that everything would be just fine?

No.

No way.

Lucas walked into the main part of the African store and saw Fatima carrying the baby. Gini looked cute dressed in a blue-and-red African fabric with her head wrapped in a polka-dotted cloth. He knew it would be easier just to leave Gini with the Senegalese woman, but his heart told him otherwise. And his heart had been a pretty good guide so far. He took Gini from Fatima and said thank you.

One of Lucas's greatest strengths was his map memory. He literally knew the streets of Paris like the lines on his hand. More than that, Lucas had a catalog of other maps in his head. He knew the layouts of museums, cemeteries, and even the Paris sewer system.

Since there were cameras everywhere tracking his every move, Lucas knew he had to get out of sight. He felt like he had an edge over Coach Creed, Magnus, and the others because of the maps in his head. When he opened the door, the map he needed bloomed in his mind.

The last best hiding place in Paris was under-ground in the catacombs.

THE EMPIRE OF DEATH

The catacombs would take him off the streets and off the security cameras. He would enter one of the burial chambers that tourists can visit. Then he would sneak into the closed areas, go dark for a couple of hours, and come out later. This time he knew he would be running from Magnus and his guards *and* from Coach Creed.

Holding Gini almost like a ball, Lucas ran, dodging cars and buses. His heart felt like it might explode. Then he remembered a shortcut. And it was close.

The gravesites of Montparnasse Cemetery looked like miniature stone houses with iron gates. The concrete vaults lined both sides of the gravel paths, allowing for the least amount of light. About halfway into the cemetery Lucas heard voices coming from somewhere. He and Gini stepped into a little tomb house.

The inside of the concrete crypt was stale. The guy had been dead for at least a hundred years. No living person had set foot in the tomb vault in at least a decade. A plastic bouquet of flowers on the floor was drenched in dust.

On his tippy-toes, Lucas peered through the iron bars in the window to see if he could tell where the voices were coming from. He eyed two men in ratty clothes who, sitting on the tomb of Samuel Beckett, seemed to be waiting on somebody. Farther down, some women were taking photographs of Man Ray's tomb.

Gini picked up the plastic bouquet of flowers and shook the dust. As the sound of boots crunching on gravel grew closer, Lucas scooped the baby up, opened the gate, and hurried down a long pathway to the edge of Sartre's tomb.

"Huis clos," said Lucas as he read the sign. "That's bad luck," he said.

Gini said, "Baaad."

"Could be," said Lucas. "*Huis clos* is a book. In English it's called *No Exit.*"

It took less than ten minutes for him to find the next ominous sign. They walked up the sidewalk, hugging the stone wall of the cemetery, and then crossed the street. Lucas scratched his head, trying to read the writing.

Gini dropped the bouquet of plastic and dusty flowers. Then she aped Lucas by scratching her head.

The sign above the door was written in French. It read: ARRÊTE ! C'EST ICI L'EMPIRE DE LA MORT.

"That means," he explained to Gini, "'Stop! It is here the Empire of Death.'"

With the map of the catacombs now fully formed

in his head, Lucas pushed open the door and dropped into the burial chamber. A long screech echoed down the corridor and bounced off a distant wall. As the door slammed shut, the echo faded in a faraway dead-end tunnel.

He scored one point for himself. He had successfully lost Magnus and everyone else. Now he needed to exit the other side of the catacombs and get to the Curukian safe house to find his sister and friends. This was the most important thing in his life right now.

Lucas and Gini walked deeper into the catacombs, and it became darker and darker with each step. They passed a group of Italians laughing and squeezed past a German family with wide, white eyes. Before long the sound of Lucas's shoes grating on the sandy floor was the only noise. The air in the next passageway was crisp and dry. Lucas and Gini stopped under one of the few light bulbs hanging from the ceiling, and Lucas's eyes adjusted. In the distance a door slammed shut.

Lucas squeezed Gini to his hip and took off as fast as he could. He didn't even look where he was going. Light bulbs flickered overhead, giving Lucas a sense that the walls were breathing. It didn't take long before they were in the darkest part of the tunnel. He stopped and froze. His pupils swelled and his heart pounded in his throat.

The walls in the tunnel were made of bones—human bones, thousands of them—all piled neatly on top of one another.

Lucas couldn't allow himself to get scared. Not now. He had to keep thinking about everybody else. He knew the only way these weird bones wouldn't freak him out was if he touched the wall. Slowly Lucas ran his palm across the bones.

Gini copied him. "Ohhhhh," she moaned.

They were surrounded by thousands of dead people: millions of bones stacked from floor to ceiling. Thick arm and leg bones formed the base of the walls. On top of this mountain of large bones, about two feet up the wall, were the smaller bones of the arms and legs, followed by the tiny ribs.

Lucas pushed deeper into the burial chamber. He and Gini crept down the corridors, past blocked-off areas, over broken barricades, through sections that were pitch-black. Dirty water began to drip from the skulls in the ceiling above their heads.

They came to a dead end lit by a tiny light bulb.

Some skulls stuck out farther than others. On one wall, a grouping of heads formed an X. In another section, the skulls formed a cross on its side. He couldn't help but wonder about all these people and why they had been buried here.

Lucas sat and leaned his head against a skull. He and Gini would be off the grid for a couple of hours. He closed his eyes and waited.

He might have dozed off, but it wasn't long before he was startled by a sound somewhere close by.

"Everyone else is cooperating," Magnus said, his voice sounding hollow in the cave.

"Yeah," Ekki said, "looks like you dropped your bouquet of flowers, too."

"Lucas," Magnus said. "There's only one way out of here."

For most people that was true. Lucas knew the main door was the only official exit. But Lucas also knew there was a tunnel that connected the catacombs with the Paris sewer system. In his brain he overlapped the two maps. The only thing left was to find the opening.

He read the graffiti on the wall. Written in charcoal on the top of a skull were the same words he had seen in the cemetery.

Lucas muttered, *"Huis clos."*

Gini said, "No exit."

Lucas looked at the little girl like she was the smartest kid ever. "You're right, but the sign's not. There's a sewer tunnel just behind these skulls."

Lucas put Gini on the ground and removed several skulls from the wall until he could see sunlight. A long and constricted tunnel led straight to a manhole in the street. Lucas heard city sounds of people talking and walking and cars honking coming from the street above. He removed a few more skulls so he could see the passageway. That was when he saw the real problem.

The opening through which they had to pass was

lined from top to bottom with skulls—cracked, mossy, rotten human heads. He could still hear Magnus and Ekki talking and getting closer. He picked Gini up and started crawling into the cranium cave. Gini held on to Lucas's neck like a baby monkey on its father. Lucas followed two small beams of light coming from the sewer cover. The air became murky with a putrid stench, as bugs of some kind ran in and out of the eye sockets of the skull floor.

A minute later Lucas muscled the manhole cover out of the way. He pushed Gini's bottom up and set her on the street. Cars honked and swerved. Lucas climbed from the sewer, snatched Gini up, and slid the manhole cover back into place. Then they dodged the traffic and headed to the sidewalk.

At the next intersection Magnus's words came back to him: "Everyone else is cooperating."

Lucas knew it had to be a ploy or a lie or both. Sophia's instructions had been "If all else fails, get to the safe house."

But that was yesterday. Or the day before. He couldn't remember.

It struck Lucas that if he went to the New Resistance safe house, no one would be there, because they had been captured by the Curukians and the Good Company guards. Coach had said Astrid and Jackknife and all the others had been taken to the Curukian safe house.

But which one?

CHAPTER TWENTY-THREE

Hervé had said you had to watch out for *le . . . le . . .*

At the next intersection Lucas and Gini came to a metro station. They went down the stairs. Lucas re-memorized the metro map and bought a ticket with the euros from his father's change bowl. For thirty-eight minutes he and Gini rode the purple line toward the Sacred Heart Basilica neighborhood, where Lucas hoped to find his sister and friends at the closest Curukian safe house.

HOSTILE HOSTEL

With Gini sitting on his shoulders, Lucas left the metro and marched on, knowing that he was doing the right thing. He passed the famous red windmill at the Moulin Rouge and headed into the neighborhood.

The farther he went up, the more the neighborhood went down. The near-midday sun baked bags of trash that had been ripped to shreds by dogs. Broken wine bottles and half-burned cigarette butts littered the cobblestone street. Block after block, graffiti tagged the doors of nameless concrete buildings. Lucas followed his instincts and moved quickly up the street. He turned another corner and spotted a charred car smoldering on the curb.

This was it.

Across the street and sitting on the stoop of a dilapidated building was a group of Curukians.

In all the commotion Lucas's internal compass had still brought him to the very spot where he needed to be.

"Curukians," he said to Gini.

"Cookies," Gini repeated.

Lucas laughed.

Gini hiccupped.

He thought Gini was so much easier to talk to than Astrid, or any girl for that matter. But he was also sure he needed to get her something to eat or drink.

"I don't want to be stupid, Gini. But if I just walk up there, they won't know who I am. Will they? I could just pretend I'm lost and ask directions and check things out that way."

"Tupid."

"Stupid?" Lucas said. "Did you just call me stupid?"

Lucas smelled stale smoke. Cigarettes. He turned around and there they were, corralling him in.

It was strange to see these boys up close with their thin and scrawny arms and tattooed hands. The mustaches they wore were shaped more like crescent moons of dried chocolate milk than actual hair. They seemed particularly bothered by Gini sitting on Lucas's shoulders.

"We're lost," Lucas said. "Can you help us get to the nearest bookshop?"

"Bookshop?" The boys laughed.

"We don't read," said a boy with a tattoo on his face.

At the back of this group of maybe a dozen boys, Lucas spotted the boy who had been in the van at the Globe Hotel. The one with the scar on his neck. Lucas pretended not to notice.

The other boy Lucas recognized from the van spoke up. "Maybe. . ." he said. "Maybe you want to ride the Good Bus with us?"

Gini mumbled, "Busball."

Gini's voice freaked the boys out and they all took a step back.

The boy with the scar said, "Let's take him in with the others."

The lobby was stale and dark—an old run-down hotel with broken lights and pieces of furniture scattered about. The boy with the scar led the group, and he shoved Lucas and Gini up the stairs. Lucas started cataloging. The banister was missing almost half of its wooden posts. He considered using the broken hand-rail to fight, but there were too many boys and too few railings. At the third floor a huge dog chained to the wall clawed at a door. The mastiff went wild with barking as they walked past.

Lucas remembered Hervé's warning: "You have to watch out for *le . . . le . . .*" Hervé must have meant, "le dog that will eat you alive."

How quickly things had gone wrong. He needed the two double agents, the boys he recognized, to help him.

The Good Company, Lucas thought. *Think opposite.*

He had to help *them* help *him*. Lucas knew there was only one thing he had in common with all these boys. Soccer. Lucas had watched every game of the last World Cup, but he certainly didn't know every player on every team. He didn't know the goalie for Team France or how well the guy played. But Lucas did know that the boys would either have something to say about the goalie, or they would make something up just so they wouldn't get left out of the conversation. It was a guy thing.

From the landing between the third and fourth floors, Lucas spotted a sign for the roof access. Now was the time. Lucas looked at the boy with the scar and hoped he would help.

Lucas said, "What's the deal with France's goalie?"

The arguments lit like fire. Talking over one another, each boy gave his opinion on France's goalie. It was a perfect diversion. The boy with the scar on his neck stopped the group on the staircase, and the boys yelled their opinions.

"He's great," Lucas heard one of the boys say.

Another said, "He stinks!"

"What about that time when he—"

The boys went at it, arguing and pushing each other down the stairs. Holding Gini tightly, Lucas slipped—unnoticed—up to the fourth floor, opened the access to the roof, and locked the door behind him.

A MEETING OF THE MINDS

Lucas Benes stood at the edge of the hostel's roof, staring down five floors to the junkyard behind the Curukian safe house. The fourteen-year-old pulled Gini close to his side. If his sister and friends were actually in this hostel, he couldn't possibly leave them behind.

"Think before you act." Lucas muttered Coach Creed's words as he searched for a solution.

A few gutters and downspouts looked promising, but with Gini it would be too dangerous to climb. On the rooftop there were several air vents, a skylight, and an old TV antenna. Attached to the antenna was a clump of cable.

Lucas knotted a quick idea.

Without a carabiner or harness, he would have a hard time rappelling from the roof. He put Gini on the gravel rooftop, and she poured handfuls of pebbles on her legs. Lucas knelt and started weaving pieces of the cable together using sheet bends. He tied a series of butterfly knots into the main line, making loops that he would use as rungs of a ladder. He hitched one end of the cable to a solid pipe on the chimney and tossed both ends over the edge. The cable landed exactly where he wanted—directly outside the room where the dog was barking.

Lucas unraveled Gini's polka-dotted headdress and tied the baby to his chest with the fabric. He then tested the cable's strength. They weren't the best knots he had ever tied, but he wouldn't need them for long. Two floors. With Gini clinging to him, he stepped over the building's edge.

Lucas's heart skipped a beat as he set one foot after another into the butterfly loops. At the fourth floor he looked in the window. Nobody.

He could hear trains leaving the nearby station and someone knocking on wood. As he lowered himself into the next loop, he heard the door to the rooftop stairwell fly off its hinges and skitter across the gravel. Then he heard a familiar sound.

A tiny bell ringing.

He looked in the next window. Inside Nalini was pacing.

The bracelet bells, Lucas thought. They sounded like the one his adoptive mother had given him. *Strange. Why haven't I made this connection before?*

The cable slipped. Lucas clawed at the window. He planted his feet on the sill and put his face up to the glass, his hand blocking the glare. Sitting on the bunk beds were Travis and Astrid.

Nalini spotted Lucas and Gini outside the glass. She pointed and covered her mouth. Lucas signaled with his hand to back up. Then he bounced his shoes off the wall and swung out wide. He tensed up and swooped in toward the glass.

His shoes hit the window's frame, and the pain shot through his hips and up his spine. But the blow snapped the old frame from the building. The whole window, glass and all, crashed onto the floor. Part of him was glad that he didn't have to break through the pane. It wasn't sugar glass.

On the roof, a clump of Curukians was now tugging on the line. Lucas stepped on the sill and into the room. He grabbed the other end of the cable.

"Double half hitch," he said, and yanked on the cord.

The cable unfurled and fell to the ground.

Travis looked at Lucas and said, "Double half hitch—slipped."

"What are you doing?" Astrid asked, staring at her brother.

"What does it look like?"

"Lucas?" Nalini said in her soft Indian accent. "Are you okay?"

Lucas handed Gini to Nalini as he moved from the pile of broken window glass and sat on one of the beds. He checked his arms for shards and splinters of wood but found none.

"Yeah," he said. "I'm okay."

"I can't believe it," said Nalini, now holding the baby. "Lucas with the baby Gini?"

Travis didn't say anything. He just kept looking back and forth from the broken window to the door, where the dog was barking wildly.

The ceiling light shed a dull yellow glow into the hostel's sleeping quarters. Shoved against the wall were six bunk beds with wool blankets. Jackknife and Astrid's housekeeping uniforms were on the floor next to a full ashtray. A computer in the corner cycled through its screen saver of pictures of Siba Günerro. On the wall a wooden sign read NEVER FORGET: RAFFISH, CURUK.

Lucas stood up and almost hit his head on the top bunk. "How did you get here?"

Nalini explained. "Robbie sent Travis and me to the Abri café, where the Curukian boys thought we were the two of you."

"As if," said Travis, flipping his long blond hair to the side.

Nalini went to finish the story. "They threw us in this black Citroën car—"

Travis cut her off. "Wait," he said. "That car was a piece of junk, and the reason they threw us in the car in the first place was because Nalini had just broken five Curukian noses."

"What?" Lucas said.

"Yeah," Travis finished. "Five Curukians surround-ed us, and then Nalini went nuts on them, kicking them all in the face. I had to crouch so she wouldn't hit me! There was blood everywhere. Then like ten guys threw us in a car. They nearly broke my arm, and they stole our phones, too."

Astrid moved a piece of glass with her foot. "So how did you find us?"

Lucas explained. "Coach Creed told me that you were all being held by Ms. Günerro because she wanted smart kids," he said. "And the Curukian safe house near the Sacred Heart was the closest."

"Lucky guess," said Astrid.

Travis smiled. "When you're lucky all the time like Lucas," he said, "it's not luck."

There was a pause as the foursome tried to shape what to do next. Lucas had figured out where his friends were but hadn't really planned what to do once he found them.

He looked at Nalini and Travis.

"I thought you two were staying on the airplane," said Lucas, confused.

Travis shook his head. "We were until the fire shut down most of our communications."

Nalini adjusted the baby on her hip. "But then Kerala went missing, and Robbie sent us to find out what was going on."

Astrid scoffed. "That girl's always missing."

Travis added, "I wouldn't be surprised if she's doing 'Good' work."

"Wait, wait," said Lucas. He fired off a round of questions. "If we're all okay, then why is Coach Creed aborting the mission? And where's Hervé? And where's Jackknife? And—"

Nalini waved her hand slightly, and the bells on her bracelet rang. "Let's slow down," she said, "shall we?"

The Indian girl's accent had such a calming effect that Lucas finally understood why his dad sent her out with so many groups. It was like yoga. Nalini didn't talk that much, and she never gossiped, but she had a way of keeping everyone focused on the work they had to do. And the bells were magical.

Astrid looked like something had desperately gone wrong. "We don't know where anybody else is, except Jackknife."

"What's the deal with him?" Lucas asked. He looked around the room. "Where is he?"

Nalini's eyes watered and Travis hung his head.

"They took Jackknife to the ceremony," said Astrid.

The way Astrid said "ceremony" scared Lucas to death. He knew exactly what ceremony they were talking about, but he was hoping for a different answer.

"Coach was right," Lucas said. "It's B-Day."

THE TRUTH BEHIND THE LIE

Outside the door the mastiff exploded in a rage of barking. The door creaked open, and a boy stepped into the dorm room. He pushed the dog back with his foot, tossed a huge bone into the hallway, and quickly shut the door. The boy's bloodshot eyes stared at them.

Lucas spotted the scar on his neck.

"So glad to see you again, Lucas," the boy said.

Travis, Astrid, Nalini, and even Gini turned to face Lucas.

Astrid snapped. "You know him?"

"Well. . ." Lucas said. "Well, yes and no. I mean . . . we've met before."

Travis looked at the boy and then at Lucas. "Go ahead . . ." he said.

"We met yesterday. Or the day before. I don't remember," Lucas said. "But these guys dropped Gini off in the Globe Hotel parking lot."

"Why didn't you tell us?" Astrid asked.

"Because," the boy said, "the only way we can help you is if we remain a secret within the Good Company."

"What?" Astrid said.

"Let me explain," said the boy. "We don't have much time—apparently Lucas unplugged the cable TV, and the other boys are upset."

"Sorry," Lucas said.

The boy with the scar explained. "I was born in Burma in a Good Hospital, and I've worked for the Good Company all my life," he said. "But I always knew I was different. For some reason I was never brainwashed like the others. I just followed everyone else and acted like they did. Then when I was twelve, I started disrupting different Good Company operations. Slowly at first. Breaking machines. Starting fires. Little things. Then I learned about Mr. Benes and the Globe Hotel and the New Resistance, so I started helping you and your group, but from within."

"Like right now," said Travis.

"Exactly."

"Burma is beautiful country," said Nalini as she shifted Gini to her other hip. "Don't you want to go back home?"

"Yes, it is nice," said the boy, "but I have no home or family, and Burma has a lot of problems right now."

Astrid used a soft voice. "Are all Curukians from Burma?"

"Most boys in this house are from Somalia and the Horn of Africa. But we have one from Waziristan, one from northern Yemen, a few from the Good Hospital in Tierra del Fuego. One escaped from Camp Fourteen in North Korea."

Travis sat on the bed and watched like he was taking notes in his mind. Then he asked, "So why are you all here in Paris?"

"We all have experience."

Astrid snapped, "In what?"

"We have all worked on pirate boats," the boy said.

"Pirate boats?" Travis asked. "In Paris?"

"Yes. Ms. Günerro loves boats and has many here in Paris," said the boy. "On the Seine."

"Where have you worked on pirate boats?"

"From time to time, we attack ships in the Gulf of Aden and sell the cargo. . . ."

"Oh my," said Nalini. "Sophia's parents were killed in the Gulf of Aden by pirates."

Once he had asked a question, Travis wouldn't stop until he got answer. "So why Paris?" he asked again.

"Ms. Günerro tells all the boys that Paris will make us rich," the boy said. "I don't believe her. The kidnappings will make *her* rich."

From the hallway they heard the dog barking again.

"So what do we do now?" Travis asked.

"The first person in your group," said the boy with the scar, "has probably been drugged already. And he is ready for the second part of his ceremony."

Astrid eyed the Burmese boy. "Where exactly is this ceremony?"

"At the Notre Dame Cathedral."

The mastiff was now growling and lunging at the thin space underneath the door. The dog broke into another round of fierce barking as footsteps approached.

"Is there another way out of here?" Lucas asked.

The Burmese boy with the scar knelt and lifted a floorboard. The hole revealed a room on the second floor, some sort of office. No one spoke. Lucas grabbed hold of a floor joist and dropped into the room below. Like a trapeze artist, Travis took Gini, hung her upside down, and lowered her to Lucas. Within seconds Nalini, Astrid, Lucas, and Travis were in the second-floor office looking up at the ceiling.

The Burmese boy looked down and said to them, "I'll keep everyone on this floor until you leave." Then he slid the board back into the floor above their heads.

THE DATABASE

The room they found themselves in was an office with old maps on the wall, white binders full of pictures, and a filing cabinet riddled with bullet holes. The paint on the walls was peeling, and the air smelled of wet concrete. An old computer hummed and rattled on a desk littered with papers.

Lucas and Gini went to the door.

"Wait," Nalini said. "There's tons of data here."

"She's right," Travis said as he threw a chair under the door handle to lock it. "It's too good of an opportunity."

Nalini began rifling through stacks of papers on the desk, scanning the documents for information.

Astrid flipped through a white binder. "Look at this," she said. "Magnus had this same kind of binder in Ms. Günerro's hotel office. They have pictures of everybody. They know everything about us!"

Travis sat at the desk. "They know way too much," he said. "I'm going to check in with Robbie."

Travis pulled his hair back as he logged in to the New Resistance website.

"The question is," Astrid said, "if the boy that knows

Lucas is working as a double agent . . ."

"Then," Nalini said, "is there someone in the New Resistance doing the same?"

"Exactly," Astrid said.

"Kerala?" asked Travis, as he stopped typing for a second. "She's always missing. And no one's seen her since she dumped Jackknife."

Nalini took Gini and let her play with the bracelet bells.

"I saw Emerald, the new flight attendant," Lucas said, "texting on the plane. Maybe she's in on something."

Travis continued typing. "Ah. Finally. Here's Robbie," he said. "Lucas? Robbie wants to know if you still have a Good Hotel master key card?"

"Yeah, I have the one we used to open all the doors in the Good Hotel and it stopped the video too," said Lucas, touching his back pocket. "Why?"

"He said the bus requires two key cards to operate. So don't lose it."

"What bus?" Astrid asked.

Nalini added, "Are we taking a bus?"

Gini said. "No Busball."

"What did she say?" Astrid asked.

"She's been saying that all day," said Lucas. "I don't know what it means."

Nalini looked at Gini. "Little baby Gini knows something?"

"No Busball."

"How would the baby Gini know something anyway?" Nalini said.

"She couldn't know anything," said Astrid, opening another binder. "She's been with Lucas all day."

"Except," said Lucas glumly, "except when she was with Ms. Günerro and Mr. Magnus when they had her at the hotel."

"Tell us, baby Gini," Nalini said. "What does Busball mean?"

"Uh-oh," Travis said. He looked up from the computer. "Robbie said the Good Company has reported Gini as kidnapped."

"Uh-oh," Gini said.

Travis read Robbie's next message. "He said the Good Company has alerted the French police that the New Resistance is responsible for the kidnapping, and the police are now looking for anyone related to the New Resistance."

"Tell him," said Lucas, "tell him we've got a Brainwashing Ceremony to go to."

Travis typed and then said, "Robbie said Coach was beyond mad that you left without him this morning. They said for everyone to get to the Shakespeare and Company safe house first. The Good Company gave our pictures to the police."

Lucas added, "But nobody has my picture."

"Not true," said Astrid. She showed the binder of photographs to the room. "We made the book too!"

Lucas saw the picture Magnus had taken in the

Lucky Office earlier in the day.

"Dang," said Lucas. "They are fast."

"Which means," said Travis, "that *we* are the data in their database."

"I look terrible in this picture," said Astrid. "Especially wearing that housekeeping uniform."

"They are awful pictures," Nalini said. "Of all of us."

"Yeah, right," said Travis. "We really should complain to Ms. Günerro next time we see her." He raised his voice. "Oh, Madame Günerro, please let us retake our binder pictures. My hair wasn't right—"

Someone tapped on the floor above their heads. Three times. Hard. Everyone went dead silent. Travis quickly logged off the website. Lucas moved the chair from the door and peeked into the hallway. Without saying a word, Nalini and Gini and Astrid and Travis followed Lucas. They scurried down the three flights of stairs and out the front door.

From the stoop Lucas looked left. "Our next problem," he said, "Jackknife and the Brainwashing Ceremony."

"That's not our problem right now," said Astrid pointing in the opposite direction. "Those two motorcycles are."

RIDING ON THE METRO

Astrid hurried the group behind the row of parked cars and away from Magnus and Ekki. Lucas figured that Goper must still be nursing his wounds from the fall he'd had the day before. At the end of the street Travis pointed at a metro sign. Lucas glanced back at the hostel.

Charles Magnus stood alone at the top of the steps. He was shaking his head and scanning the street. A group of Curukian boys stormed out the front door of the hostel and surrounded the chief security guard. Magnus pointed toward Lucas, and the boys took off running.

Nalini and Gini led the group—Astrid, Travis, and Lucas—around two more corners, where they flew down a flight of stairs and into a metro station.

Lucas handed Astrid some of the euro coins. While Astrid bought the tickets, Lucas checked the map again. They clicked through the turnstile, ran through the subway station to the platform, and boarded the next metro to the center of Paris. The train, Lucas knew, would take them to both the safe house *and* to the Notre Dame Cathedral, where

Jackknife was presumably being brainwashed at that very moment.

The train car was brightly lit and oddly quiet. A few French girls giggled, but most of the riders were reading or napping. No one said anything. Lucas used the time to refuel his mind.

At Les Halles, the central station of Paris, they changed trains. Clumps of people got off with them and poured into the waiting areas. The smell of sweet crêpes and Nutella filled the air, and music echoed in the tunnels. A grunge guitar screeched from one passageway. Another corridor amplified bongo drums, and still a third made like a mega-phone for a woman singing opera. The four teen-agers and the eighteen-month-old snaked their way through the maze of hallways, past movie posters, and down the flights of stairs to the train platform that would take them to the safe house.

The wall posters were enormous, big as a two-car garage. One was for Disneyland Paris, another for Air France, and a third was a perfume ad of a woman in her underwear.

Travis shook his head. "Ooh la la."

Gini copied him. "Ooh la la."

A hot wind blew through the station as the next subway train approached. Passengers moved toward the edge of the platform . . . everyone except four unhappy-looking boys in black mock turtlenecks standing at the bottom of the stairs, talking on phones. At that same moment two French police officers entered the waiting area from the opposite direction.

Cops. Curukians. Coach Creed.

Everyone was now after them. Lucas couldn't believe it. Or maybe he could. He just wanted to stop and explain everything to them all. But no one would listen. That much he knew.

Within seconds Lucas envisioned the metro map and changed plans. They would have to walk—run—to the safe house.

The corridor he chose smelled of fresh coffee. Nalini's bells echoed off the subway's tiled walls and added to the intensity of the day. As they corkscrewed through the small canal-like hallways, noises seemed to come from everywhere and nowhere. An electric guitar. A man yelling. The movie posters on the walls began to repeat, and Lucas wondered if they were running in circles. From somewhere behind them there came the sound of boots slapping the concrete.

Lucas didn't know where the noise was actually coming from, so he just kept doing what he had learned from climbing. *Keep moving up,* he coached himself. It got hotter and hotter as they ran deeper and deeper into the network of hallways. Signs read M, RER, T, and RATP.

Nothing meant anything.

They were moving so fast when they came to the turnstiles that they glided over them, one by one.

The up escalator was broken. They stamped up the thick stairs to the crowded plaza. Lucas had the feeling of walking into bright sunlight after watching a dark movie mid-afternoon. Completely lost.

POMPIDOU

The square was so crowded that Lucas was sure the security camera on the opposite wall would miss them.

At least he was hoping it would.

Lucas had to figure out what was going on. Fast. Part of him started to feel guilty for leading everyone to a place he didn't know. He ran the day through his mind, trying to figure out how he had gotten to this very spot. Maybe he had actually caused today's troubles. His father's words came back to him: "Just do the thing that has the highest value at any given moment, and you'll be making the right choice."

Lucas took a deep breath. "We've got to find Jackknife."

"No," said Astrid. "We've got to get to the safe house."

Lucas wasn't about to argue. He knew he had the best map of Paris in his mind. He also knew he would have to lie to his sister to save his friend.

"You win," said Lucas. "Follow me."

Lucas was determined to move through the crowd. He cut through the mass of people and the others followed. Boys were skateboarding over a Roman wall that surrounded a patch of grass. A group of school kids ate Big Macs. And two mopeds cut through the crowded plaza, buzzing uncomfortably close to Nalini and Gini.

Travis caught up with Lucas and walked with him to the edge of the next plaza. A weird-looking building covered in multicolored pipes stood opposite them. The moped circled back and parked next to Travis. Lucas was part excited and definitely part suspicious when he saw who the riders were.

Astrid spoke first. "Kerala! Sora! What are you doing here?"

"Robbie and Sophia sent us," said Kerala. "He spotted you on a video feed, coming out of the metro."

Sora added, "There's a group of Curukians following you."

"Yeah," Kerala said. "We'll keep them occupied while you get to the safe house."

Lucas was really itching to go now. "This is the Pompidou Center," he said to Travis. "Isn't it?"

"Yeah," Travis said, "which means we're close to the bookshop. Right?"

"And," Lucas whispered to Travis, "the Brainwashing Ceremony at Notre Dame."

"We're not going, Lucas," said Astrid sternly.

Gini giggled loudly and they all turned to see where she was pointing. A shirtless clown hopped up on a wooden box in the middle of the giant square.

He shouted in English with a strong French accent.

"Maybee," he said, "it iz not hot enuff for you here in Paree?"

Diversion, Lucas thought. Perfect.

The clown struck a match and lit a juggling baton on fire. He balanced the stick in the palm of his hand and then dropped it. Faking every move, he picked up the burning baton, pretended he had burned his hand, and whimpered toward the crowd like a puppy.

In his Frenchy English he said to a young woman in the crowd, "You are a guud-looking woman. Kiss my burned hand, pleeease."

There was a chuckle from the crowd as the woman kissed his hand and the clown jumped for joy. Next he drank from a plastic bottle, and his mouth swelled with the liquid. He blew kerosene across his lips and through the burning baton. The flame flared over the crowd and there was a big gasp.

The clown approached another woman. "You are a beautiful woman. Kiss my burned lips, pleeease."

As soon as he had gotten his peck on the lips, the clown strutted away like a proud rooster. Gini, now sitting on Nalini's shoulders, clapped her chubby hands. Then the clown tossed the burning baton high into the air, and it flipped over and over until it floated down. The clown spun himself around and opened the back of his baggy pants. The burning baton dropped straight into the back of his underwear.

The clown went nuts. His legs danced in the air,

and he started slapping his pants to put out the fire. Then he screeched a long, hound-dog wail as he looked sheepishly at the crowd.

"A kiss?" he begged. "Pleeease!"

Everyone laughed and clapped and put money in his hat on the ground. On the other side of the crowd four boys in black mock turtlenecks were not laughing.

"We got them," said Kerala as she put her helmet back on. "You guys get to Madame Beach's safe house. Sora and I'll meet you there."

Sora and Kerala hopped on the mopeds and buzzed across the plaza toward the Curukian boys. Lucas, Astrid, Travis, and Nalini and Gini wormed through the crowd and stopped at the weird statues spraying water in the Stravinsky Fountain. Lucas looked back to see if Sora and Kerala were really slowing the Curukian boys down. Kerala was slouching with her arms around two of the boys.

Lucas thought, *Curukians must like Goth makeup.*

"Which way to the safe house?" Astrid asked.

Lucas lied. He wasn't going to the safe house. He was going to the Notre Dame Cathedral to save Jackknife before his friend's brain was washed into Curukian mush.

A NEVER-ENDING SUPPLY OF CURUKIANS

Astrid punched the crosswalk button with the side of her fist, and they waited for the light to change.

Travis was the first to spot the boxy black car that had picked him up earlier. The Citroën eased up to the intersection and stopped at a green light. As the doors opened, the newest, freshest Curukians hit the streets. These boys carried bricks, and as they passed a parked car, one of the boys smashed a window. The car alarm screamed into the street, and everyone turned to look.

Lucas was impressed. The tactic was a perfect distraction. He knew that if they didn't react quickly, they would be surrounded and would never get to Jackknife.

From the left six more Curukians walked down the sidewalk. Behind them three Curukians stood blocking the passage back to the Pompidou Center.

Traffic in the street came to a screeching halt. Pedestrians stopped and stared. As the crowd focused on the car alarm, Lucas pushed his sister into the street. Travis and Nalini and Gini quickly followed as they ran through the maze of now-stopped cars.

Horns blew to move the traffic jam as the New Resistance kids hid behind a car.

Six very tall Curukian boys in black uniforms climbed on the stalled cars. They moved in a simultaneous wave as they marched and stomped across the roofs and hoods. A boy with dragon tattoos on his arms and neck knocked the heel of his boot on the windshield of a student driver's car. Then he kicked the sign on the roof advertising the auto school.

The hairs on the back of Lucas's neck tingled. Each time he ran into these Curukians, they seemed to be bigger and meaner. The boy pointed at Astrid's head, which was now poking up from behind a tiny Smart car. Without moving his eyes, the tall Curukian boy bolted across the cars, hopping from hood to roof.

Lucas ran to the Smart car, where he came eye to eye with a skinny woman in the passenger seat. As she stared at the Curukians marching toward the car, her white knuckles clutched a fat bottle of Perrier. It was the best tool he had. Lucas rammed his hand through the open window and ripped the water bottle from the woman.

It took no time for the tall boy to leap across the line of cars. He moved fast and kept his dark eyes fixed on Astrid. Nalini and Gini scurried around the traffic jam of cars and made it to the other sidewalk. Travis sprang into his jujitsu stance, ready to fight right there in the street, but it would be useless against these boys. They were giants.

The tall boy jumped, hurdling an entire car, his legs spinning in midair. At the same time Lucas backhanded the bottle of Perrier across the Smart car's side-view mirror. Fizzy water and green glass sprayed across the hood, covering the car with a thin slippery layer. When the tall Curukian boy landed on the hood, his boots hit the wet broken glass. In a near-perfect back flip, his body turned under him as he crumpled to the road with a painful thud.

The other Curukians gathered round the boy lying in the street, as if waiting for instructions. It seemed that if one fell, the others somehow lost the ability to think for themselves. Lucas glanced down at the boy. Bloody nose and mouth. Probably a concussion. Lucas could tell the boy was breathing and would be fine, but still he felt really bad for tripping him like that. It was a cheap trick. And he didn't like having to use it.

Police sirens screamed from all directions: *beedoo, beedoo.*

A split second later Nalini and Gini led the others down the sidewalk, past the tourist shops, and through the crowds of people. They tore into the section of town called the Swamp. It was a fitting place to throw someone off their scent, or so Lucas hoped.

CARNIVAL OF THE ANIMALS

The kids sprinted as fast as they could, past the Picasso Museum, past the toy stores, the candy shops, the Jewish delis, and the security cameras. There was no one following them, but they ran anyway. They ran past eight hundred years of history in about eight minutes.

They stopped under some scaffolding and caught their breath. Nalini then led them through an archway and into the place des Vosges. And there Travis and Lucas collapsed on a bench between rows of roses. Astrid plopped down on the ground as Nalini set Gini in a patch of grass. The baby crawled around for a second and wiggled her diaper. Then she farted.

Still standing, Nalini dropped her head into her hands. "I don't know who's helping and who's not."

"I don't know how many times I need to say it," said Astrid, "but we need to get to the safe house."

"We're going," Lucas said.

"What's that?" Travis asked, squinting his eyes. "Music?"

"This, you mean?" Nalini said, jingling the bells for Gini.

"No," said Travis.

Someone was playing music. Violins, flutes, xylophones. Travis stood and peeled back the branches of the bush. Standing around the fountain was a band playing the *Carnival of the Animals.*

"My mom would have loved this music," said Astrid longingly. "She played that song about a million times when I was a kid."

"We are kids," said Nalini.

There was a long pause as they all seemed to be lulled by the music. Nalini sat in the grass with Gini and let her play with her jewelry. Astrid stretched out on the grass, while Lucas and Travis leaned back on the bench like they were sunbathing. Lucas closed his eyes. The melody made him think that they might actually be too young to do what they needed to do.

"Hey, Lucas?" Astrid said.

"Yeah."

"Thanks for coming back to the hostel to get us. You didn't have to do that."

"Not a problem," he said with his eyes still closed.

"Hey, Lucas?" Astrid said again, her voice soft.

"Yeah."

"I think it's great that you got that rappel at the hotel right."

"Thanks."

That might have been the first compliment Astrid had ever given Lucas. There was nothing better than having a sister or brother believe in you. It made

Lucas feel great, but somewhere inside, he felt like he still owed Astrid an apology.

There was no better time than now.

"Hey, Astrid?" Lucas said.

"Yeah," she said, sounding a bit like Lucas.

"I'm sorry about your mom," he said.

"Yeah," said Astrid, "me too." They were all quiet for a second. "It wasn't your fault, Lucas. Our mothers died for a reason. For a secret. My mom didn't just go down to Tierra del Fuego to adopt you and those other eight kids. There was something bigger going on."

Suddenly Lucas was very awake and refreshed. Enthusiasm for more success poured through him. He hopped up and ran the options through his head. A crazy cast of characters began to populate his brain. Ms. Günerro. Magnus. Curukians. But the strongest feeling filled his heart.

Lucas announced: "We still have to get Jackknife."

"What about the safe house?" said Astrid.

"I have to agree with Astrid here," said Nalini. Her Indian accent seemed highlighted. "We could use some assistance."

"Jackknife can't wait," said Lucas. "I'm going to Notre Dame, and I'm going to help my friend. I'm not going to allow something bad to happen if I can prevent it. You can come with me, or you can go your own way. Either is fine by me. Really."

Lucas invested what he now thought was precious time waiting for his sister and friends.

Travis always seemed to know when to be funny and when to be serious. He looked at the girls. "If you were Jackknife, in that situation, about to be brainwashed, wouldn't you want—wouldn't you expect—your friends to come help you?"

Everyone nodded.

Travis continued. "We might all be kids here, but that doesn't mean we have to sit back and always ask grown-ups for help. At some point we have to rely on ourselves."

"I just don't want anyone hurt," said Astrid.

Lucas was adamant. "At least we will have tried."

NOTRE DAME IS OUR LADY?

Holding Gini tightly, Astrid trotted up behind the group. "I'm coming with . . ." she said.

Astrid seemed to be trying extra hard to understand what was going on. She was always smart in school, but dealing with unreasonable people at the Good Company had confused her.

"Sorry," said Astrid. "I'm just a logical person, I guess. I like empirical evidence to make decisions. Not gut reactions."

Lucas felt better knowing that Astrid and Gini were coming along. They were going into the belly of the Notre Dame Cathedral to confront Ms. Günerro and her Brainwashing Ceremony. Lucas knew they could always use Astrid's smarts, and Gini had been a good-luck charm since he found her. They would need every bit of luck available.

They left the safety of the park, but everyone looked confident. Astrid even seemed less worried for the first time all day. She ran into a pastry shop by herself and bought croissants for everyone, which were a huge hit. Lucas retold the funny story of Gini pooping green-pea diarrhea on Goper. Travis was laughing so hard that his croissant came through his nose. Lucas also told them about meeting Coach Creed in the African shop, and they all had a good laugh at how much trouble Lucas would be in when they got back. Astrid told Travis and Nalini the story about searching the Good Hotel rooms and seeing people in their underwear. They laughed like crazy.

Then they crossed the Seine onto an island in the middle of Paris, where they quickly lost that fun feeling. They were close. And they knew it.

The back streets had a distinct smell of water. Lucas's mind swirled with ideas of how to re-kidnap Jackknife, but none of his plans seemed any good. The river made him think of a getaway by boat, but he didn't have a boat. And swimming in dark river water scared him to death. They crossed another bridge onto the next island. They crept through the shadows of the famous flying buttresses, which, like giant arms, held up the walls of the eight-hundred-year-old Notre Dame Cathedral.

In his mind there was a tiny flicker where Lucas considered running away from everything. A voice in the back of his mind called out and pushed him to focus, and not on himself. He wondered how Jackknife might feel at this very moment. His Brazilian friend had been alone for a long time and could very well be on his way to having his brain washed of all its memories. It was possible that Jackknife's brain had already been washed, and he wouldn't even recognize Lucas or any of the others. No old friends. No memories of soccer in the hotel lobby. No broken vases. He would start telling everyone he was from Raffish, Curuk, and they would be enemies.

Lucas couldn't bear the thought of it.

They came to the stone plaza in front of the cathedral, and there the nightmare called the Good Company got worse. Lucas spotted something odd on the Left Bank. The traffic became uneven and almost confused.

Ms. Günerro rode on the back of Charles Magnus's motorcycle. The pink poodle's head was poking out of a side basket, its tongue flapping in the wind. From the Left Bank they crossed the Petit Pont, going the wrong way on a one-way bridge. Cars and delivery trucks pulled to the side as the motorcycle split the traffic. Magnus parked the motorcycle on the plaza in front of the cathedral doors. In a flash Ms. Günerro and the poodle rushed through the front doors of the Notre Dame Cathedral.

A Günerro sighting confirmed the fact that something bad was definitely about to go down.

Astrid led the others through a side door to the church. There Travis seemed to know what to do. He dipped his hand in the marble font of holy water and made the sign of the cross. They all copied Travis.

Beams of sunlight streamed through stained glass windows and bathed the cavernous cathedral in a cool blue light. Tourists shuffled around, staring at tombs and statues and praying silently in pews. A small classical band was setting up for practice in the south transept, and the organ piped in echoes of medieval music.

Four Curukians entered the cathedral. The boys dipped their hands in the holy water and then started flinging it on each other. Lucas and the others followed Astrid down the side aisle toward the front. They stopped when they saw someone who could surely help them.

A priest entered from the dressing quarters wearing a long black robe. He curved behind the main altar and stood in the choir chapel. He straightened his vestments, and then he seemed to signal to the four Curukians.

The boys marched down the nave, weaving around tourist crowds. They cut behind the altar and cordoned off the whole choir section with a red velvet rope. At the top of each brass pole there was a sign written in at least twenty languages.

QUIET. SERVICE IN PROGRESS.

The Curukians entered this blocked-off area and got on the kneelers encircling the minister. The priest then leaned over to speak with the boys. A white fog rose from the robe's hem.

"Oh no!" Astrid said.

Gini repeated, "Ohno."

"Not in a church," Lucas said, shaking his head.

"Oh," Nalini said. "Please."

"Guys," Travis whispered. "That's Ms. Günerro dressed up as a priest!"

The crowds were now blocking the view, so the kids moved closer. They stopped between a giant statue and a bank of prayer candles. The statue was a gruesome sculpture of Saint Denis holding his head in his hands.

Nalini glanced at the statue and then at Ms. Günerro. "This is simply too weird for me."

"I've read about this," said Travis. "Ms. Günerro likes classical music for some of her ceremonies."

"This is sacrilegious," said Astrid.

Just then the organist began to play louder, and the music flooded the cathedral.

"No," said Lucas. "This is perfect. For her. Remember what my Dad said: Ms. Günerro will do everything out front and right in your face."

"I'm lighting a candle," said Astrid. She put a euro in the coin slot and lit a prayer candle. "This is for Jackknife."

Dressed as a priest, the CEO of the Good Company raised her arms in the air and spoke to the boys now kneeling before her. As she leaned forward, her robe spurted another cloud of smoke.

"What is that?" Nalini seemed skeptical.

Astrid shook her head. "She's got that fake Freon in her dress!"

"It's dry ice," said Travis. "It's not fake Freon."

From the rope around her waist Ms. Günerro

pulled four envelopes and gave one to each boy. She stretched a smile across her tight lips and clapped her hands once. The boys rose obediently, then marched around the velvet rope and down the center of the cathedral. As they left the church, three new Curukians entered and started walking up the nave.

Lucas spotted the poodle in pink spinning circles in the back hallway.

"This way," he said, and the others followed.

While Ms. Günerro tended to the dry ice seeping from her robe, Lucas moved his group down the hallway. They walked down a long, dimly lit corridor and stopped at the door where the poodle sat. The sign read PRIVATE.

Lucas opened the door and there, slumped over on a bench, was Jackknife.

THE BRAINWASHING CEREMONY

Jackknife looked like he had just come from the hospital. His skin was ashen, his lips were dry and cracking, and his bloodshot eyes were rolling around in his head.

Lucas ran to him. "Come on, Jackknife," he said, shaking him. "Wake up!"

Travis was glum. "It's not going to work."

Nalini looked to Travis, the brainwashing expert, for an answer. "What's going on?"

Travis explained. "What I've read is that sometimes they give you a medicine before the actual brainwashing ceremony."

"A drug, you mean," Lucas said. He turned to Jackknife. "Hey, buddy. What did they give you?"

Jackknife moaned and drooled when he talked, little bubbles of spit popping on his lips. "About . . . twenty minutes after I swallowed some Good Drink, called nepenthe," he said. He stopped for a second and swallowed hard. "I felt this like . . . tingling up my spine." His breathing was forced. "Then . . . I couldn't remember." He dropped his head. "But I always knew . . . I always knew you guys would come back."

Astrid said, "Lucas is the one who really got us here. Thank him."

Jackknife said nothing. He had already fallen back into his dead sleep.

The side door to this room opened with a creak. Fearing the worst, Ms. Günerro, they all turned to see who was there.

"Hervé!" Astrid said. "What are you doing here? And why are you just showing up everywhere?"

Hervé put his finger to his lips and whispered. "Madame Günerro thinks she can control me—that I am still a 'Good' boy, but it's not true." He pointed his cane at Jackknife. "Listen. Your friend here has been drugged so that the brainwashing works better on his brain."

Astrid said, "That's what Travis just said."

"Excuse me," Nalini said to Astrid. "Do you . . . know . . . this guy?"

"Oh, yeah. Sorry," said Astrid. She put Gini on the bench next to Jackknife. "Hervé met us when we first got to Paris. Long story, but he used to be a Curukian and now he is undoing his brainwashing and helping us."

Travis suddenly seemed very interested in Hervé. "How do you undo a brainwashing?"

"If something can be learned, then it can be unlearned," Hervé explained. "Brainwashing is essentially a way of teaching or convincing your brain over time to do something in a certain way."

Travis said, "Just like when you listen to a song and it gets stuck in your head."

"Exactly," said Hervé. "Music is a form of brainwashing. But as always there is good music and bad music."

"I still don't understand," Astrid said. "Why would Ms. Günerro do the ceremony in a cathedral? It's so disrespectful."

Hervé explained, "The ceremony in the church has not worked very well, but Madame Günerro still loves it. It's the oldest brainwashing method at the Good Company. It's essentially a series of chants that she says over and over for a year until the person does exactly what she says."

"Why is the success rate so low?" Travis asked.

"Ha," said Hervé. "This is where we have an advantage. Madame Günerro doesn't know that bells can block a brainwashing. The nuns at the Good Hospitals figured this out a long time ago. This is why they often secretly give children bells. And this is why some in the Good Company are not brainwashed."

Lucas was shocked. "Astrid's mother gave me a bell before—"

"It didn't come from her mother," Hervé said, correcting Lucas. "I imagine that bell came from the nuns at the Good Orphanage in Tierra del Fuego."

Lucas looked back at Hervé, for whom he felt a little sympathy. The French boy had worked hard to undo whatever it was that Ms. Günerro had done to him.

Lucas asked, "What's back there in that room you just came out of?"

"The four altar boys."

"What else?"

"A bench," said Hervé. "Closets."

"Are the altar boy clothes in those closets?" Lucas asked.

"But of course," said Hervé.

Lucas wanted more answers. "How many altar boys does Ms. Günerro need for this ceremony today?"

"Four."

Lucas eyed his three other friends. "Let's change actors in this play," he said. "Hervé. Would you get us four robes? Quick. Please."

"You've got to be kidding," said Astrid.

"Good idea," said Hervé. He clumped on his cane and moved into the room. Moments later he returned with four robes.

"I can't believe you want us to change clothes again," said Astrid.

In less than a minute Nalini, Travis, Lucas, and Astrid were dressed as altar boys in hooded robes that nearly covered their faces.

They all looked at one another.

"Well," said Astrid. "At least it's better than the housekeepers' uniforms Lucas had us in back at the Good Hotel."

"We all look like the grim reaper," said Travis.

Suddenly there came a skin-against-skin slapping

sound. Then another slap, followed by a baby's giggle.

"The baby Gini," said Nalini.

When they turned, they saw Gini sitting in Jack-knife's lap, slapping him across the cheek with her little hand. With each slap Jackknife puttered his lips, and Gini giggled. Nalini picked the baby up.

Jackknife uttered, "What?"

And then his chin slumped to his chest.

Travis got in Jackknife's face. "Your name," he said, chanting in a monotone voice. "Your name is Paulo Cabral. Your nickname is Jackknife. Say it: I am from Brazil."

"I am from Brazil," moaned Jackknife. His head rolled back. Then he muttered, "Brazil. Home of the best *futebol* players in the world."

"That's a good sign," said Travis.

"Even though," Lucas said, "they're not really the best soccer team. Argentina is."

Travis joined in. "The Americans will win the next World Cup. No question about it."

"Hey, guys," said Astrid. "No time to argue."

From the hallway they all heard the voice that no one was ready to hear. Standing in their robes, Lucas, Astrid, Nalini, and Travis bowed their heads and shielded their faces.

Ms. Günerro didn't come into the room. "Hervé?" she called through the closed door.

"Yes, *madame*," said Hervé.

"Have the altar boys bring me Jackknife now," she

said, "before the prep medicine wears off."

"Right away," said Hervé.

"And Hervé?"

"Yes, *madame*," he answered.

"Call our safe house," Ms. Günerro said, "and have them send over the other four inductees."

"Anything for you, *madame*," he said, rolling his eyes at the foursome.

They could already hear the fading sound of Ms. Günerro's heels clomping down the hallway.

Lucas asked, "Can you keep Gini here by yourself?"

"But of course," Hervé said.

"Hervé," said Travis. "Is there some sort of code or math sequence to the bells? Like a Fibonacci number?"

"Madame Günerro is original," said Hervé. "She would never do what someone else has done before. If you want to help Jackknife, distract him with bells. That's all."

Lucas and Travis helped Jackknife to his feet. Astrid led the group out of the room and they stopped just before the altar steps in the main church. With her head down, Ms. Günerro was standing in the middle of the choir section just behind the altar.

The organ began to play.

"That's Bach," said Lucas.

"Toccata and Fugue," said Nalini.

Travis looked like he just realized something clever. "In D minor," he said pensively. "That's the key to the language."

"Well," said Astrid. "Mr. Siloti would be so impressed with all his music students."

As the organ played, Ms. Günerro stood with her eyes closed.

"I've read about this," Travis said. "If she's doing this ceremony by the book, she'll raise her arms in the middle of the song and then call us up to her."

Ms. Günerro stood several meters away from the semicircle of kneelers and chairs. A slight fog seeped from the hem of her robe as she raised her arms.

"Perfect," said Travis excitedly. "When we're on the kneelers, keep your heads down so she doesn't recognize us. Like Hervé said, ring the bells to distract Jackknife and block Ms. Günerro's message."

The organ began playing loudly, and the whole cathedral filled with church music. The tourists seemed mesmerized. Ms. Günerro signaled for the altar boys to come and join her.

"This is it," said Travis. "I can't believe we're doing this."

"I can't believe," Astrid added, "that she's doing this in a church. It's totally wrong."

"What do you expect?" Lucas said. "It's the Good Company."

The foursome helped Jackknife into a chair in the cordoned-off choir section. With their heads still bowed, Lucas and the others dropped down on the kneelers.

Over the ever-louder organ music, Ms. Günerro

spoke to Jackknife.

"You have been prepared to rid yourself of your past and embrace the Good you have within."

As Ms. Günerro spoke, Nalini distracted Jackknife by tapping him on the back with her tiny bracelet bells.

"Focus on the bells," Travis whispered to Jackknife. "Not her voice."

Ms. Günerro bent down slightly. "Lower your head and close your eyes and breathe in the Good."

Out of the corner of his eye, Lucas could see tourists trying to nose in and take pictures of the ceremony, but Ms. Günerro was too far in the back of the choir section for them to see. The head of the Good Company had chosen a perfect place, as usual. It was public, but no one could tell how evil her plan actually was.

Ms. Günerro's breathing changed to the same tempo of the music. She began to chant like a Gregorian priestess, distant and echoing, as if surrendering to the power of her own message. Then she lowered a cloth mask over her face.

With her eyes poking out two holes in the mask, she spoke in what Lucas thought sounded like gibberish. He couldn't understand what she was saying, which made it all the more frightening.

Travis winced as he worked through the translation.

"I got it," he whispered to the others on the

kneelers. "She said, 'All control is self-control.'"

The organist tore through a series of deafening chords.

Lucas, Astrid, and Nalini and Travis rang the bells next to their kneelers. Ms. Günerro didn't seem to notice the distraction. She swayed in a tight circle. Her voice was choppy as she chanted.

Travis translated. "Your mind is mine all the time."

Even though they were creepy, Lucas was amazed at Travis's translations.

Ms. Günerro raised her head high. Her whole body wavered and wobbled as she spun herself deeper into a trance. She was the most terrifying person Lucas had ever seen. This was way more than wrong. This was scary. Ms. Günerro's eyes seemed to bulge out farther from the two holes in the mask as she nattered the next incomprehensible line.

The four altar boy bells chimed, dulling Ms. Günerro's words. Travis again translated. "All who follow will believe. They are the willing and they are the free."

Ms. Günerro swooned and swayed and looked as though she might fall from sheer exhaustion. The smoke from the dry ice in her dress completely covered her from the waist down. The top half of her body seemed to float on the dry-ice cloud. The sight gave Lucas the creeps.

Travis translated again. "There will be one way and only one way and that way is the Good way."

Then Ms. Günerro lifted the cloth mask to signal

the end of the ceremony. Dots of sweat covered her face.

Lucas and the others remained glued to the kneelers, waiting for an opportunity. Through the fog there was a strange crunching sound, slow and methodical. Ms. Günerro checked the hem of her robe, most likely to see if the dry ice was leaking again. The crinkling sound grew closer.

Ms. Günerro continued with her work. She smiled at Jackknife. "You are now from Raffish, Curuk," she said. "Come and give me a hug."

Yuck, Lucas thought.

Jackknife stood obediently as the fog of dry ice began to thin slightly.

The noise returned and Lucas knew. For the New Resistance, opportunity didn't always knock. Sometimes it crawled.

In her crunching and crinkling diaper, Gini crawled onto the altar and behind Ms. Günerro. The baby pulled on the leash and the poodle in pink followed.

Jackknife stretched out his arms to hug Ms. Günerro as Gini crawled to the edge of the remaining dry-ice cloud. The poodle then stopped directly behind Ms. Günerro.

Jackknife glanced back at his friends and winked. The bells had worked. As he moved to hug Ms. Günerro, Jackknife pretended to faint and fell toward her.

The famed Siba Günerro gasped. She stepped backward, stumbled over the poodle in pink, and toppled to the floor like a giant statue. The dry ice in her dress burst, and fog started to cover the floor in the entire choir section.

Within seconds three Curukians stormed through the tourists who were now flooding the altar to get a closer look.

In the middle of the dry-ice fog, Jackknife gathered his friends.

"Get me out of here," he said. "Now!"

SHAKESPEARE IN PARIS

They fled the choir section and threw off their robes. Lucas, Astrid, Travis, Jackknife, and Nalini and Gini slipped out the cathedral's back door, through a swarm of tourists, and past Ekki and Goper waiting at the front door. They ran down the island and through a bird market, and finally came to the Pont Neuf—the New Bridge—which at more than four hundred years old was the oldest bridge in Paris.

There, they crossed the river Seine and into an insane part of town.

The Latin Quarter was the unofficial headquarters of the bohemian lifestyle in Paris, which meant anything could happen. Like the cameras watching them, Lucas eyeballed everything. Restaurants full of people lined the streets. Waiters were zipping back and forth to tables on the sidewalks. Partway down the street, a butcher carried half a bloody cow on his shoulder and into his shop.

Close by, a film crew aimed lights up toward a building. An actor, an enormous woman in a maid's outfit, squeezed her big arms through a dormer window and called out. *"Garde de l'eau,"* she cackled as she threw a pot of liquid down onto the street.

"Gross!" Astrid said.

"What?" Jackknife asked.

Astrid explained, "I think that's supposed to be the lady's chamber pot she was throwing out!"

Nalini winced. "As in poo?"

"Yes," said Astrid. "As in got to go to the loo!"

Lucas trudged on. "Let's get to the bookstore."

"And to a real bathroom," Astrid added.

Lucas's internal map told him they were close to the safe house. They rounded the next corner and saw a sign that Astrid had been begging for all day: SHAKESPEARE AND COMPANY.

They read a note on the safe house door: *Fermé.* Closed.

Lucas knocked.

Inside, an old woman set a coffee cup on a counter and shuffled to the door, her hand quivering as she fumbled her keys. She opened the door.

"Entrez," she said over the sounds of creaking hinges.

The gray-haired woman cast a cautious eye into the street and then let the children in. She shut the door quickly and locked it, the blinds clanging against the glass.

The inside of the shop was dark and musty and smelled of old books and French fries. From floor to ceiling, nearly every point was crammed with literature. Stacked on the floor and scattered on tables and chairs, there were piles of hardbacks, paperbacks, and even unfinished manuscripts. The spaces between the banister posts were crammed with small collections of series books. There was a rack of old clothes toward the back. On the top floor somebody's frilly underwear hung from a clothesline.

"I am calling myself Madame Beach," said the old woman. Her English was quite good, but her French accent was strong. "You must excuse my English for it is far too long that I am not speaking it."

Astrid and Nalini hopped as they walked toward the back of the shop.

"Excuse me, Madame Beach?" Astrid said. "Before I do anything, I need a bathroom."

The wrinkles in Madame Beach's forehead deepened. *"Excusez-moi?"*

"A bathroom," said Astrid.

It was clear that the native French speaker was confused. Madame Beach batted her eyelashes as she tried to figure out what exactly Astrid was saying.

"Bathroom?" Madame Beach said, dropping the *h*. "You want to take a batt? Are you dirty?"

"Not a bath," said Travis calmly.

"A WC," added Nalini.

Jackknife was blunt. "They have to go . . . pee."

"Ah . . . pee-pee," said Madame Beach. "You need *la toilette*. Not a bathroom."

The old woman pointed, and the girls scurried down the hallway. Travis and Jackknife milled around the store and stopped when they found an old collection of Asterix comic books. Lucas was standing still, thinking about how to get Madame Beach to take care of Gini.

"She needs. . ." said Lucas, squishing the diaper. He was too tired to remember how to say the word in French, so he said, "She needs to change le diaper."

"La couche," corrected Madame Beach. She took the baby from Lucas and whispered, "Come with me. Upstairs."

Lucas followed Madame Beach and Gini up a worn red staircase. When they got to the second floor, Lucas couldn't believe who was there.

"Dad!" Lucas said. "It's really you! It's really you this time."

Still wearing a sport jacket, Mr. Benes opened his arms and gave Lucas a giant bear hug.

"Lucas," he said. "I'm so glad you're all right."

Lucas's shoulders collapsed as he fell into his father's chest. He didn't want to move. Part of him wanted to stay right there wrapped in his dad's arms, listening to his heartbeat. But the other part of Lucas had too much to tell.

"You're not going to believe what we saw," said Lucas, stepping back from his father. "Ms. Günerro has got this like crazy ceremony and she wears this mask and chants some kind of weird language. And she gave Jackknife a drug. And she tried to recruit me and then—"

"Slow down, slow down," Mr. Benes said. He looked to Madame Beach. "I have to say hello first."

Mr. Benes turned to Madame Beach, and they lightly kissed each other's cheeks. One, two, three times, they touched cheeks. He rubbed Gini on the head.

"My old friend," he said to Madame Beach. "Thank you for everything. Again."

"Yes." Madame Beach smiled. "That makes a long time since I am seeing you. I am happy you remembered our secret entrance."

"The trapdoor needs a little oil," said Mr. Benes, smiling at Madame Beach. "How are you, Adrienne?"

"I am well."

Mr. Benes's tone changed. "We still have some work to do."

"Apparently," she said. Then she gestured toward Lucas. "Is he ready?"

"After what he's done today and yesterday," said Mr. Benes, "Lucas is most definitely ready."

"Then it is time to tell him everything we know."

Still carrying Gini, Madame Beach led the way through a small room filled with books. Mr. Benes put his arm around Lucas and followed the old French woman into a tiny apartment. Mr. Benes took Gini and changed her diaper, while Lucas went into the upstairs bathroom.

When he came out, he looked around the apartment. Behind the clothesline of old-lady underwear, there was a single bed next to a kitchenette. Dishes were neatly stacked, and a flower wilted in a glass by a window. On top of a dresser there was a collection of picture frames. Lucas felt a sudden and strange attraction to the photographs.

"Lucas, sit down for a second," said Mr. Benes. "I want to hear all about everything you've seen and done since I last saw you. But right now we don't have time."

"What do you mean?" Lucas said, taking a cane-backed chair. "We've seen a Brainwashing Ceremony. We know how she does it. Travis even knows the language!"

"That's great," said Mr. Benes as he too sat down at the little table. "But I have spent a good portion of the past two days at the ICMEC getting fresh information on the Good Company." Mr. Benes glanced at Madame Beach, but he didn't slow down. "It seems the Good Company is having money troubles. You knew they lost a multimillion-dollar contract to guard the Eiffel Tower, but as it turns out, they've also lost several other contracts worldwide, which is why Ms. Günerro and Magnus are working feverishly to find new ways to make money."

"Yeah but," said Lucas, "Robbie said earlier that the Good Company had reported earning more money than ever before."

Madame Beach grinned cynically. "Not all companies are honest."

"So," said Lucas, "that's why Ms. Günerro's going to

do a big mass kidnapping. For Bunguu?"

"Right," said Mr. Benes. "But there's something else."

Madame Beach picked Gini up, stood next to Mr. Benes, and stared at his profile. "It is what I think it is, no?"

"Yes," said Mr. Benes as he looked at Madame Beach. "You've been right since the very beginning."

Lucas couldn't keep his eyes from drifting toward the photographs on the dresser.

"Go ahead," said Madame Beach. "You want to look at those photos, no?"

Lucas leaned forward and studied the collection, cataloging every detail of every picture. The frames were different sizes and shapes, some silver and others wooden. The photographs were mostly black-and-white with an aged sepia look. The pictures had been taken all over the world: London, Disney World, the Alhambra, Tiananmen Square, Red Square, and Washington, DC.

"Do you see her?" Madame Beach asked.

"Who?"

"Your mother."

"Yeah," said Lucas, pointing at a photograph. "I recognize her picture, but she was only my mother for a day."

Lucas looked again at the picture of Astrid's mother. She was standing on the steps of the Good Hotel in Bali with a surfboard under her arm.

Madame Beach corrected him. "I am not talking of the mother of Astrid," she said. She placed her hand on Mr. Benes's shoulder. "Not this man's wife, not Kate Benes. I make reference to your mother—your birth mother, Lucas."

Goose bumps covered Lucas's entire body as he heard the words. "What do you mean?" He swallowed hard and then repeated, "What do you mean, my 'birth mother'?"

Mr. Benes walked across the tiny apartment to Lucas while Madame Beach set Gini on a blanket with a bowl of dry cereal and a sippy cup. Since Lucas had never seen a photograph of his birth mother, he scanned every picture on the dresser into his memory one more time.

"The one in the boat," said Madame Beach, now standing next to Lucas.

Lucas's arm reached over the rows of picture frames. His hand moved in slow motion as he lifted a photograph from the very back row of the collection. The picture was of a woman with long black hair sitting in a wooden motorboat moored near Notre Dame Cathedral.

Lucas stared at this picture for what seemed like fourteen years.

"She is beautiful, no?" said Madame Beach longingly.

The sound of the old woman's voice startled Lucas. He wasn't quite sure how long he had actually been staring at the photograph. Part of him couldn't believe this was a picture of his real mother, and another part of him wanted to jump inside the photograph and sit right next to her on the boat. Lucas glanced up at his father, then snapped his eyes back to the first photograph of his birth mother he had ever seen.

"You knew her?" Lucas said, touching the glass.

"We all worked together at the Good Hotel," said Madame Beach. "I hired your mother."

"You were her boss?"

"A long time ago, I was the international manager of all Good Hotels worldwide," said Madame Beach. "And I hired your mother to work at the hotel in Buenos Aires."

"To do what?"

"She was a cleaning woman."

Lucas grinned as he thought about the housekeepers at the Globe Hotel in Las Vegas.

"My mother was a cleaning lady in a hotel," said Lucas humbly. "That's so cool. Did you know that, Dad?"

"I did."

Madame Beach held on to Mr. Benes's arm. "I also hired this handsome man when he was just finished with university."

"And Kate, too," said Mr. Benes.

"So," said Lucas. "Where is she now? My mother? My . . . birth mother?"

"I do not know, sadly," said Madame Beach. "During the hotel *conférence* here in Paris, she and I shared many Good Company secrets on the boat when this picture was taken. But that was fifteen years ago. Unfortunately, Madame Günerro discovered that your birth mother was keeping a journal."

"Was she a spy or something?"

"No," said Mr. Benes. "She was just a good person who did good things. She discovered Ms. Günerro's child-kidnapping network a long time ago, and she kept notes in her journal."

"So what happened after Ms. Günerro found out?"

"After the *conférence*, Madame Günerro changed the Good Company. She sent many women employees into hiding—Tierra del Fuego and Senegal, in particular."

"And you just let them go?"

"Madame Günerro is very strong," the old woman explained. "If we were ever going to help them, we knew that we had to save ourselves, first. So, I quit my position with the Good Company, and I hired your father again, and Kate, too. We started the Globe Hotel together. And with your mother's information we secretly started the New *Résistance* to stop Madame Günerro and to find these lost women like your mother."

This was the best story Lucas had ever heard.

"Which brings us to today," said Mr. Benes. "Today at the ICMEC, I learned that your mother—your birth mother—discovered some other illegal activities at the Good Company."

"More than kidnapping?"

Mr. Benes breathed deeply. "The ICMEC has proof that Ms. Günerro has been embezzling money—stealing—from her own company for years. Before your mother found out, Ms. Günerro had moved billions—not millions, but billions—of dollars, yen, euros, and every kind of stock and world currency into secret hidden accounts."

"My mother was a cleaning lady," said Lucas. "Why would she know anything about the hotel's money?"

"Because," said Madame Beach, "she took out the trash. And people's secrets are always in the trash."

"To make a long story short," said Mr. Benes, "your mother found out about these accounts and had the money moved into secret accounts somewhere else in the world. And then she changed all the account numbers and pass codes."

"So she stole stolen money?"

"Not exactly," said Mr. Benes. "She didn't steal it. She transferred the money to stop Ms. Günerro from kidnapping and putting more children to work."

"But," said Madame Beach, "we do not know where it is located—the money, the codes, or the accounts."

"What do you mean?" Lucas looked at both adults standing before him. "So nobody but my mother knew about this money?"

"There have always been rumors in the New *Résistance*," said Madame Beach, "but never proof of this large sum of money."

"The problem has always been," said Mr. Benes, "that the account numbers and all the codes to all the accounts were supposedly destroyed in the ferryboat accident that you were in."

"What?" Lucas said, still somewhat skeptical.

"You see, Lucas," said Madame Beach. "When your mother arrived in Tierra del Fuego, she was about to give birth to you. And she knew that as soon as you were born, Madame Günerro would take her away and torture her to make her tell where she had hidden the money. Your mother wanted to protect you. So she gave you to the nuns, and she called me to have you adopted." Madame Beach then smiled sweetly at Mr. Benes. "I naturally called John and Kate to adopt you."

"Kate and your mother," said Mr. Benes, "had been good friends at the Good Hotel, which is why Kate went to adopt you. And not me."

Lucas was desperately trying to piece this story together. "So my mother gave the codes to Kate, and they were lost when Kate died on the ferry."

"We had always thought that your mother had given Kate the codes," said Mr. Benes. "But the ICMEC believes that the nuns at your Tierra del Fuego hospital gave the codes not to my wife—not to Kate—but actually to you."

"Me? I was only a baby. I didn't have them," said Lucas. He paused. "Did I?"

"No," said Madame Beach. "Impossible."

Gini crawled between the group and untied Mr.

Benes's shoes.

"Weird," Lucas said. "Ms. Günerro said today that Kate Benes stole very important account information from her, and she said that those numbers died with her."

"Madame Günerro was lying to you," said Madame Beach. "She was testing you to verify what you knew."

"Because," said Mr. Benes, "the ICMEC told me today that Ms. Günerro believes that you have always had the numbers and the codes."

For the second time that day Lucas's brain ran through every number he had ever seen in his entire life. This time he actually came up with a few possibilities. Still holding the picture of his mother in his hand, Lucas stared at his father and Madame Beach.

"Maybe that's why Ms. Günerro wanted me to join her company," said Lucas.

"What do you mean?" Mr. Benes asked.

Lucas explained. "We were in her office earlier today. It was freezing. And she made us a proposal to either be brainwashed or work with the Good Company. She tried to make it seem like we would be safe if we worked for her. It was really weird."

"Interesting," Mr. Benes said. "Ms. Günerro knows something we don't."

"So," said Lucas. "How do I find out about my mother then?"

"I do not know if she is alive or not," said Madame Beach. "Unfortunately there is probably only one person who could tell us where she is."

Everything became clear to Lucas. "Siba Günerro," he said.

Mr. Benes looked at his adopted son. "Are you okay with this?"

"I've waited my whole life for this," he said. "I just didn't know it."

Madame Beach batted her eyes. "You know where to go?"

Lucas was ultraconfident. "There's only one place that Ms. Günerro would try to pull off a mass kidnapping."

In his heart, he made himself and his mother a promise. Lucas set the picture frame back on the dresser. He looked down at Gini and knew he had to leave her. He picked Gini up, gave her hug, and handed her to Madame Beach. He could actually feel a lump in his throat. It didn't feel right, but he knew it was the logical thing to do. Then Lucas shook the thought from his head, focused on what he had to do, and flew down the staircase.

"Everybody," he announced, "listen up. I want everybody to change clothes."

"What?" Astrid argued.

Travis chuckled. "The fashion police strike again."

Nalini joked. "Is *la France* rubbing off on you?"

"Not now, guys," Lucas fired back. "I know what I'm doing. Put some Frenchy clothes on so we don't stick out."

Astrid seemed shocked by Lucas's tone of voice, but she copied Nalini and stepped behind a rack of clothes. Lucas joined Travis and Jackknife behind a stand of dress shirts.

The clothes on the hangers had been there so long that they had gone out of style, and back in, without ever having left the store. Astrid and Nalini seemed to be having a fabulous time free-shopping. They nearly fell over each other laughing. While Astrid flashed a pair of hippie pants, Nalini held up a velvet dress for everyone to see.

"Talk about vintage," said Astrid, who grabbed another pair of striped bell-bottoms. "Look at these!"

Lucas knew Jackknife and Travis were not normally into shopping for clothes. They threw on the first things that fit and stepped into the middle of the room. The boys were all dressed in dark T-shirts, gray Pierre Cardin canvas pants, and brown leather shoes. Lucas took the two key cards from his old pants. There was the Globe Hotel key card and the one Boutros had given Astrid in the Good Hotel, and Gini had reactivated it. He put both cards into his back pocket.

The girls looked like Parisian postcards. Astrid wore a Hermès striped blouse and a black Chanel skirt with a small slit in the side. She spun around to show it off. Ever the fashion queen, Nalini wore a black lace dress from LaCroix with black Lobb sandals, and of course her signature bells on her wrists.

Madame Beach held Gini and they looked down

over the railing at the two girls.

Gini said, "Ooh la la."

"Madame Beach?" Lucas called upstairs. "Do you still have that boat?"

"But of course," said the old woman.

Lucas stared at the traffic outside the bookshop's front window. "I need a key."

Madame Beach leaned over the railing. "Who knows how to drive a boat on a river?"

"I do," Jackknife said confidently. "I grew up on the Amazon."

"Follow the river east," said Madame Beach. "Descend the third staircase and you will see my boat. The key is inside the flagpole."

"What's the name of the boat?" Astrid said.

Madame Beach winked at Lucas. "*Le Secret*," she said.

THE RIVER SEINE

In their new old clothes, the five kids stood outside the Shakespeare and Company bookshop.

"This feels odd," said Astrid.

"It does," said Nalini.

Jackknife shrugged. "What? Free clothes?"

"No," said Nalini. "Not having the baby Gini with us."

"She's part of our team," Astrid said as the two girls looked at each other.

Nalini didn't miss a beat. She bolted back into the bookshop, and within a minute she returned to the group with Gini in her arms.

"I don't know about you," Nalini said, breathing a little heavily, "but I just love this little girl. She makes me so focused. Because she's a baby and all it makes what we're doing that much more important. You know."

"Then let's go," Lucas said.

The five kids and one baby flew down the street past a blur of graffiti. By the time they reached the wall bordering the river, the sun had almost set.

Street traffic was whizzing by, and boats were

puttering up and down the river. The kids walked under the plane trees lining the sidewalk, where clusters of booksellers peddled postcards and miniature Eiffel Towers. Just past the booths, a class of art students sat at easels, painting copies of Monets, Renoirs, and Pissarros.

Gini reached out for one of the postcards.

"Man," said Travis. "That *steak frites* and French fries was so good."

"Dude," said Jackknife. "*Frites* are French fries."

"When did you guys eat?" Lucas asked. "I'm starved."

"Mr. Beach was cooking in the back of the bookshop," said Jackknife.

"Really nice fellow," said Nalini.

Astrid glared at her brother. "Where were you that whole time, Lucas?"

"Um . . ." Lucas hesitated. "The upstairs bathroom."

"The whole time?" Astrid said, crinkling her cheeks.

"Yeah."

"Well," said Astrid. "It's pretty obvious you and Madame Beach have some secret."

"Right," said Nalini. "What was that wink she gave you, Lucas, when she told us the name of her boat was the secret?"

"Yeah," said Travis. "What was that all about?"

Lucas had to think quickly. He couldn't tell them what he had just learned about his mother. Not just yet. That was *his* mother, *his* secret. He wanted to hold on to the idea of his mother by himself for a little while. All on his own.

Some secrets should be kept secret. But he also had to be honest with his friends.

Lucas picked up one of the Eiffel Tower key rings from the booth "My dad, Mr. Benes, was upstairs meeting with Madame Beach. They think the Good Company is losing money, and they think Ms. Günerro is desperate."

Travis and Jackknife nodded, but Lucas could tell his answer didn't satisfy his sister.

"Okay," said Astrid, putting a postcard back. "But we don't even know where we're going?"

They glared at Lucas.

Without looking, Lucas returned the key ring to its peg and ran the map of the city through his head.

"They told me that Ms. Günerro is still planning on kidnapping a group of kids to sell to Bunguu. But knowing Ms. Günerro, she'll do her work not in a dark alley, but in the most obvious places. And in Paris, there's only one place."

"That's obvious," said Travis. "But they lost the contract to guard the Eiffel Tower."

"Wait," said Jackknife. "They're having a carnival there tonight. Right?"

"The lady likes an audience," said Travis. "If you haven't noticed."

"Brilliant," said Nalini, laughing to herself. "Perfectly brilliant plan."

"It is perfect." Astrid shook her head. "Sick but

perfect. Isn't it?"

There was a strange calmness when they got to edge of the river. No one was behind them—no Curukian boys or Magnus or guards. No police. No one even noticed when six kids climbed into the baby blue seats of a boat named *Le Secret*.

Madame Beach's boat was gorgeous. It was a 1967 Italian-made Riva with a mahogany hull and shiny teak decks. Lucas untied the boat from the dock, hitched the ropes around the brass cleats, and pushed the boat back. Briefly he caught his reflection in the dark water and shuddered at the prospect of falling in. A memory of an explosion flashed in his mind. He hoped Jackknife really knew how to drive a boat.

Jackknife cranked the V-8 engine, spun the motorboat around, and cut into open water. Astrid, Nalini, and Gini moved to the back of the boat, and the murmur of the motor quickly lulled Gini into a nap. With the wind in his hair, Lucas stared back at the girls and envisioned his own mother sitting at that very spot, fifteen years earlier.

As night settled over the Seine, Jackknife flicked on the running lights and sped through the dark water. Lucas and Travis leaned over the front windshield. The City of Lights was brightly lit, but the river water was murky and ominous. Darkness worried Lucas the most. He hated the idea of their boat crashing and of having to swim through cold black water. He glanced around, hoping to spot a life jacket or at least a Styrofoam ice chest. But there was nothing left to save them.

They glided past barges, water taxis, and sightseeing boats. Lights decorated the angles of flyboats, and cameras clicked as tourists gazed in amazement at all the sights. Jackknife powered the little boat past the Paris beach, the famed Louvre museum, the place de la Concorde, and the Grand Palais. They rounded a bend in the river, and that's when they saw it: the highlight of any Parisian cruise—the Eiffel Tower.

Lit by thousands of lights, the Eiffel Tower was ablaze in electricity.

Gini opened her eyes. "Ooooooo," she cooed.

They tied Madame Beach's boat to a floating dock between two enormous barges, and everyone got off the boat, except Jackknife.

"I'll stay," he said.

Travis asked, "Are you all right?"

"Yeah," said Jackknife, who still looked a little pale. "I'll turn the boat around in case of a water evacuation."

Astrid seemed calm, like she knew everything would be fine. She looked to Lucas. "Which way, Map Boy?"

Lucas pointed, and Astrid led the others across a busy street bordering the river. For a second Lucas slowed down and checked behind him. He spotted Coach Creed, Robbie, and Sophia climbing out of a van. Plan B was in place, just in case. Lucas quickly

caught up with the others. They ran into a neighborhood and hurried down trash-filled lanes where cats
screeched from behind parked cars. From a lighted
apartment window above their heads they could hear
a piano playing jazz and a woman cackling loudly.

Like floating moons, big white streetlamps lit the
Champ de Mars. Good Company Security officers
with German shepherds patrolled the pathways of
the wide, grassy park leading to the Eiffel Tower.
To the east Napoleon's mausoleum hid in shadows.
To the west the Eiffel Tower dominated the skyline.
Straight ahead there was a giant carnival.

"*This* is the place," said Lucas.

CARNIVAL

Underneath the canopy of trees sprouted a make-shift village of white tents bustling with excitement. Boys and girls in colorful costumes were throwing spears across hedges. Jesters, fire-eaters, and jugglers clumped together in small packs to rehearse their acts. Next to the Eiffel Tower there was a collection of jumping castles, a rappelling rope, and an enormous slide sloping down from the tower's first floor.

"We should do that slide," said Travis. "On a board."

"You sound like my brother," said Astrid. "But we're not doing that."

"I guess," Lucas said, "we can't do the climbing wall and rappelling rope either."

Astrid didn't even answer. She, Nalini, and Gini cut straight across the park toward the Eiffel Tower. Lucas and Travis followed. They all formed a tight line through a thick crowd, weaving their way up the midway, where tents were decorated with international flags. Banners on top of the tents popped in the wind, and the air smelled of cinnamon and crêpes. There were kids everywhere. In the opposite direction there were bumper cars, candy grabbers, and coin pushers. Lights flashed and bells rang. Lucas couldn't help but think how fun it would be just to stop and play games. The other side had a Velcro wall, sumo wrestling, and a bungee run. Sounds from a Western shooting gallery snapped like firecrackers, and Gini cried out at the noise.

"Ohhhhh," she breathed. "Pow."

"Jackknife would love this," said Astrid. "This is like . . . like *Carnaval* in Brazil."

"This *is* a carnival," said Travis.

Nalini started to say something to Travis but yawned instead.

The group followed Astrid through a mob of excited carnival-goers. Groups of Belgians wearing black, yellow, and red robes were racing on stilts while little kids ran underneath their wooden legs. The side alleys were dotted with arcade games and food trailers. Popcorn. Cotton candy. And French fries with mayonnaise.

Through all the noise, Lucas recognized a voice.

"Guillotine!"

The boy he and Astrid had seen the day before was playing with his cardboard guillotine.

"Yeesss!" He said. Then in his bad fake French accent, he called out, "The blade is cardboard. So you get the sensation of . . . *whack!* . . . without the blood."

The boy continued to raise and lower the cardboard blade over a mannequin. He beckoned down the midway in an attempt to get others to play at his booth.

"Marie Antoinette, Louis Says, Simon Says."

Opposite this guillotine they all spotted the juggler from the Pompidou Center doing his same routine of tossing burning batons into the air. Everyone suddenly seemed strangely familiar.

Travis, who was walking ahead of the others, came to a full stop. "Step right up," he said, mocking a carnival voice. "Get your peach-fuzz mustaches! Right here. Get them while they last."

"Yeah," said Lucas. "I see them too. Two o'clock. Ten o'clock."

"You're right," said Nalini. "There's a Curukian manning every booth."

The group now moved slowly as they kept an eye on the Curukians. At most carnivals, the games were rigged to help the carnival people. This fair was the opposite. Every player was actually a winner. At the ball toss they were practically giving away balls. It occurred to Lucas that if all these boys, these Curukians, were brainwashed to work for Ms. Günerro, then they could just as easily be brainwashed to recruit other children. Maybe all the booths were recruiting centers, secret back doors into the Good Company.

At the next intersection they came upon a massive group of ball-toss winners. Hundreds of kids carrying balls—soccer balls, American footballs, rugby balls—were streaming up and down the midway. Lucas scanned the group and recognized no one. Astrid and Nalini spotted several kids they had hoped not to see.

"Oh no," said Astrid. "There's Kerala!"

"And Sora," said Nalini.

"And that little Terry kid," said Astrid. "The one from the airplane who wasn't supposed to leave. Robbie is going to be mad at him."

Before they could say or do anything, they had to move out of the way.

Coming down the main midway was a parade. A Dixieland band and a mob of carnival revelers dressed in the wildest costumes danced in the lane, parting the crowd to the sides. It was *Carnaval*, Mardi Gras, and New Year's Day all in one.

Men in white masks and frilly costumes led the main group. They threw so much candy and confetti that it looked like snowfall. Kids in the crowd went crazy, scrambling for bonbons. Behind this group, tall women dressed in elaborate gowns covered in reflective sequins, rhinestones, and colorful pheasant feathers pranced through the carnival street. A line of parade floats with cartoon characters and space-men followed the dancers. Then a troupe of flagged trumpeters marched in and introduced the Carnival Queen.

Beams of light began crisscrossing the midway in anticipation of something big. Nalini and Astrid were speechless. They stood with their mouths and eyes wide open as they watched the final costume entering.

The queen's dress was part gown, part parade float.

Four Curukians held the skirt of a flowing lace dress that fanned out, its hem floating on motorized wheels. The dress was entirely covered in tiny mirrors and rhinestones, white and silver with flickers of blue. In the center of this floating dress and partially hidden behind a glittering mask was Siba Günerro. Ostrich feathers two meters tall sprouted from Ms. Günerro's headdress, while diamond-like wings soared behind her. A single move of her hand gave the impression that she was breezing through a field of falling stars.

The CEO of the Good Company smiled and waved brightly as she presented herself to the crowd as Carnival Queen and Mistress of Ceremonies. She began to play a small piano keyboard in front of her, and she filled the night air with Beethoven's Fourth Symphony. The crowd went crazy for it and gathered around Ms. Günerro, clapping and dancing along with her as she parted the sea of people.

"That is absolutely gorgeous," said Nalini as she held Gini up to see.

Astrid nodded reflexively. "It's the most beautiful dress in the world."

"Right, right," said Travis. "I mean who wouldn't like a dress that's part truck."

Lucas had long since stopped watching Ms. Günerro and focused his gaze on the Eiffel Tower. He'd known Ms. Günerro would eventually show up, but he couldn't believe how ridiculously over-the-top this lady was. She would of course do anything to get her way—with kidnapping and brainwashing at the top of her list.

Lucas spun around with the others and watched the parade fade down the midway. Off to the side he recognized a sign.

BUSBALL.

A greeting in twenty languages read A WINNER EVERY TIME.

Lucas turned to the group. "Busball," he said.

"Busball," said Gini.

Lucas nodded. "That's what she's been saying all day!"

"Noooo. Busball," said Gini.

Lucas understood. He marched straight up to the tent and threw open the front flap.

"Lucas!" said a familiar voice. "But of course."

CHAPTER 37

A NEW WAY TO KIDNAP

The others peeked inside the tent and said at the same time as one another, "Hervé?"

"But of course," said Hervé, his French accent as thick as ever.

The inside of the tent smelled like exhaust, like bus diesel fuel. Hervé was sitting on a weird throne-like chair, by himself, surrounded by tiny kindergarten chairs.

"Welcome," said Hervé with a wink. "Welcome to the Busball."

Astrid didn't wait for an explanation. "What do you think you're doing, Hervé? You just show up everywhere. Like out of nowhere."

Lucas, Travis, and Nalini and Gini stepped behind the group of tiny chairs.

"No. No," said Hervé. "Madame Günerro found me in the cathedral, and she completely believes that her brainwashing over me could never be undone."

Lucas yanked on his hair. "Astrid! Don't be rude," he said. "Hervé doesn't have to convince us every time we see him. So far he has been helpful, and that's good enough for me."

The smart side of Travis got serious. "Exactly," he said. "So then what's going on here, Hervé?"

"First you must know that Madame Günerro has many . . . um . . . brainwashing methods. The Busball method is drug-free and uses a video, which prepares brains for future brainwashings. Like the drugs that were given to Jackknife." Hervé scanned the group. "Where is he? Where is Jackknife?"

Lucas knew Hervé was being as honest as possible. "He's waiting on our boat back in the river."

"Be careful," Hervé said. "Madame Günerro has many Curukian boats on the river Seine. Boys from the Horn of Africa. They play police, you know?"

Lucas was anxious to move on. "So what is this Busball?"

"No Busball," echoed Gini.

"Why all the balls?" Travis asked. "The footballs and all that."

With his head buried in his chest, Hervé seemed ashamed, but he explained anyway. "Before the kids watch a *vidéo* on the bus, they are each given a ball. Or they 'win' a ball. A football, an American football, cricket ball, any ball they want. A microchip is embedded in each ball to track the children with GPS and to locate them when Madame Günerro is ready for them."

"She tracks them?" said Nalini. She scoffed. "Absolutely sick!"

"We've got to go get the others," said Astrid. "That

little Terry kid won't stand a chance by himself."

"I agree," said Lucas. "How do I get on the next bus?"

"No. No," said Hervé. "Once on the bus, you are locked into a seat. You will never escape. At this moment now Magnus is loading the children with Busballs onto the bus."

Travis shook his head. "I've never read anything about Busball."

"It is new," said Hervé.

"Oh great!" Travis said. "A new way to kidnap!"

"But of course," said Hervé.

"There's no new way to kidnap," said Astrid. "They kidnap the kids, then brainwash them. Simple as that. Right?"

"No," said Hervé. "Just the opposite."

"She brainwashes them," said Travis, "so she can kidnap them?"

"Correct," said Hervé. He explained wholeheartedly. "The plan is to brainwash a group with a light version tonight, and then in a month or so, using the Busball—the toy ball—Madame Günerro and the Curukians will find these children and re-brainwash the same group for a deeper level of commitment to the Good Company. That way you cannot erase the ceremony like I am trying to do for myself." Hervé seemed anxious. "Their methods are much too complex now."

Outside the tent there came a huge burst of noise

as the crowd cheered and screamed. Lucas peeked out of the flap to see what it was. Fireworks were exploding over the carnival.

"Let me get this straight," said Astrid. "The kids get a ball, get on the bus, watch a video, and then they just go home tonight and think nothing has happened to them?"

"Exactly," said Hervé.

"It's like stupid smart," said Lucas.

"Yeah it is," said Travis. "If you're brainwashed, then you won't know that you've been kidnapped."

"Madame Günerro," said Hervé, "has always believed that kids will cry when kidnapped, unless of course they've been brainwashed beforehand."

"Brainwash, then kidnap." Nalini shook her head at Gini. "Backward but brilliant."

"Brilliant," said Ms. Günerro as she flung the back flap to the side. "Did I hear my name?"

Lucas closed the front flap and swallowed hard. Astrid and Nalini and Gini got up quickly, and Hervé stood nervously next to Travis, who was tugging on his long hair.

Ms. Günerro had been separated from her float. She was now wearing a glittery dress, which, with the slightest movement, made the blue and silver gems sparkle like icy water. Her face was still mostly hidden behind a rhinestone mask. The Good Company CEO stepped into the tent with Magnus, Ekki, and Goper whose face and arms were heavily bandaged from the fall he had had the day before.

In typical dramatic fashion Ms. Günerro announced, "I have Good news and I have Good news." She chuckled. "The Good news is that it's time for Busball!" She paused. "The other Good news is that Mr. Magnus here tells me that he has only one seat remaining on the Busball bus. One seat for one lucky winner."

Astrid, Lucas, Travis, Hervé, and Nalini and Gini stood like statues and said nothing.

"Come now," said Ms. Günerro, eyeing the kids from behind her mask. "You're fleeing from your fears; I will help you embrace your fears. Trust me."

Hervé looked like he might get sick. Astrid and Travis seemed so frightened that they held hands. Nalini squeezed Gini.

Lucas was torn. He wanted to find out about his mother and her secret—if there really was one—but he also wanted to help the kids on the bus. Finding his mother was his own private mission, but he would have to get close to Ms. Günerro somehow, someway, to find out the truth. Like it or not, Ms. Günerro was at the core of all of this. Standing there in the tent, Lucas couldn't possibly know what searching for his mother might uncover or if looking for his mother would help or hurt the kids on the Busball bus. Either way, this was his only chance.

Ms. Günerro lifted her mask and squinted at Lucas. It became obvious that the mask was also a pair of prescription glasses. Then Ms. Günerro reached her hand out into the air and pretended to pull a name from a hat. "Let's see who we have here." She unfurled an imaginary piece of paper and read, "Lucas Benes has been chosen for Busball!"

"No Busball," said Gini.

"Tell that little boy to be quiet," snapped Ms. Günerro. Then she smiled at Lucas. "It appears that Lucas's number has been chosen."

"No. Don't take Lucas," said Astrid. Her voice didn't have her usual sharp tone; instead she sounded somewhat sly and deceptive. "Take me," she said. "You'll be disappointed in him. He's way too nice and always does the opposite of what you think is right. He can out-think anything you throw at him. If you try to brainwash or kidnap him, he'll constantly change, and he'll always be one step ahead of you. How do you think we got here to this Busball before you? It's because of Lucas. He's street smart."

Astrid seemed almost proud and jealous of Lucas at the same time. She may not have completely learned how to do or say the opposite with Ms. Günerro, but her tone in this rambling speech was just confusing enough. Astrid had finally come to trust her little brother. And that was big.

"No." Astrid shook her head. "Take me. I'm like my mother. What did you call her? VP? Very picky? Well, I'm a very picky rule follower." She gestured to Travis and Nalini and Gini. "We're all rule followers. Order us to do something, and we'll do it exactly how you told us to do it, even if it doesn't make sense. And it seems to me that everything the Good Company does doesn't make any sense. So pick me. Pick us. Not him."

"Now that's the hunger I've been looking for!" said Ms. Günerro, showing an eerie sign of happiness. "What's your little name again?"

"Astrid Benes."

"How adorable," said Ms. Günerro. "Let me guess. You're his sister, aren't you? Don't want your little brother hurt, do you?"

No one has ever liked being invisible to other people.

"Did you forget my name?" Astrid glared at Ms. Günerro. "Maybe you've washed your brain of its intelligence."

Ms. Günerro was now visibly shocked. Magnus moved closer to Astrid as if trying to intimidate her while Ms. Günerro put her mask back on.

"Let me tell you a story," said Ms. Günerro, obviously trying to change the subject. "You know, they always say that blood is thicker than water, that family is the most important thing. I disagree. I had a brother once, and he was jealous of my Goodness and my Good Company success. Yes, in a rage, he called me on the phone one day. The day I buried my mother at sea, in fact. He called and said, 'I hate you and I never want to see you again.' Which was fine by me. I took all of his stock, his money, everything that he had with my Good Company, and I gave it to children in need—until someone changed the account numbers, that is."

"You don't make any sense," said Astrid. "Why not take me? Why does it matter who you take?" Then the tone of her voice became extra stern. "Why exactly do you want my brother?"

"So glad you asked," said Ms. Günerro. She took off her mask again. "Your brother is a thief. He stole several high-value numeric codes that belong to me."

Travis came to Lucas's defense. "Lucas is not a thief."

Nalini showed Gini off. "He saved this baby."

"I placed that baby in my Good Orphanage Vancouver and Lucas stole her. He's just like his mother. A pretend do-good thief."

"But," said Astrid. "His birth mother is—"

"Enough from you," said Ms. Günerro cutting her off. She turned to Ekki and Goper. "Take these girls out. I think I hate girls more and more every day."

Ekki and Goper did as they were told and grabbed Nalini's and Astrid's arms.

"All three girls," said Ms. Günerro, pointing at Travis.

"I'm not a girl!" Travis said.

"That long hair," said Ms. Günerro, "makes you look like a girl."

Again Ms. Günerro pointed at Travis. "Take her and the others up the Eiffel Tower. Now!"

"Oh yeah," said Goper. "We can ride that slide now."

"Shut up." Ekki slapped him.

As Ekki and Goper led Astrid, Travis, and Nalini and Gini through the back of the tent, Ms. Günerro re-fixed the rhinestone mask over her eyes.

"Oh, you too, Frenchy," Ms. Günerro said to Hervé. "I don't need a half-brainwashed, part Curukian, crippled Frenchman." Her voice became serious. "All I need are the numbers this Lucas boy is hiding."

Hervé scurried around the tiny chairs and quickly followed the others out of the tent. When he opened the flap, Gini crawled inside and squatted on the ground.

Lucas now stood directly in front of Ms. Günerro and Charles Magnus, feeling like he was about to get expelled from hotel-school. But for some reason, he felt a little stronger with Gini in the tent with him.

"I didn't do anything," said Lucas.

"My friends," said Ms. Günerro softly. "My friends at the ICMEC tell me that you have my account numbers."

"I don't have them," said Lucas with defiance. "End of story."

Magnus stepped back so he was standing next to Ms. Günerro. "Did Kate and John Benes actually adopt you—with signed papers—from the Good Hospital in Tierra del Fuego?"

"Yes," said Lucas. "Actually just Kate. John adopted me later. To be perfectly accurate."

"So," said Ms. Günerro. "You would have been on

the ferry when it crashed?"

"I was."

"Impossible," said Magnus, who was shaking his head. "How could you have possibly survived that ferryboat accident? It exploded and everyone died."

"Hush, Chuckie," said Ms. Günerro. "If it is true that this boy was on that ferryboat, then this boy could only be . . . Lucas Kapriss."

"Lucas Kapriss?" Lucas said. "No, I'm Lucas Benes."

"The son of Señora Luz Kapriss. Head of House-keeping at the Good Hotel Buenos Aires," said Ms. Günerro. She analyzed Lucas's face. "I can see her in your eyes now."

"And you lied to us," said Magnus. "You said that John Benes had been divorced. But John Benes never remarried, so he couldn't have been divorced."

"You said it," said Lucas. "Not me. I just didn't correct you."

"To me," said Magnus, "Lucas looks like that Peace Corps volunteer in Senegal that we had so much trouble with. Ken Creed."

"We'll know everything we need to know in a short time," said Ms. Günerro confidently. "We will have full access to all of Lucas's memories."

Ms. Günerro nudged Magnus, and the head of Good Company Security grabbed Lucas by the arm.

"Come on," said Ms. Günerro. "Life on the other side is going to be a lot brighter for you."

"Fine." Lucas picked Gini up. "But I'm taking her

with me."

"Oh," said Ms. Günerro. "How did that little boy get in here?"

"She's a . . ." said Lucas. "Oh forget it." It wasn't his job to teach Ms. Günerro the difference between a boy and a girl.

Ms. Günerro asked, "Has the baby cried yet?"

This had to be a trick question. Lucas thought back to the Globe Hotel parking lot. Gini had cried. Several times. On the motorcycle when Magnus thumped her.

Lucas knew exactly what Ms. Günerro was doing, so he invented another answer. "No," he said. "She's never cried."

"That's because he's already been brainwashed into being a Good Baby." She shrugged. "Brainwashed babies are better."

Then Magnus parted the flap at the back of the tent and led Lucas and Gini and Ms. Günerro to the Busball bus.

BUSBALL

The black bus with tinted windows was dark and packed with kids. All eyes were glued to headrest monitors. Lucas looked down the aisle to see if he recognized anyone. Sitting in the middle of the bus were Kerala and Sora. He flashed a wave, but they didn't seem to notice him at all. In the way back, Terry sat on the edge of his seat watching his screen. The only remaining spot was a single jump seat catty-corner to the driver.

Ms. Günerro smiled gleefully as she boarded the bus. She took her place in the driver's compartment, which looked like a small airplane cockpit. A control panel with flashing buttons and blinking lights surrounded the driver's seat. On the dashboard there was a silver card reader with two key cards sticking out. This was much more than just a tour bus. This was a Good bus, a go-anywhere, amphibious brainwashing-kidnapping machine.

Magnus briefly hopped onto the bus and told Lucas and Gini to sit in the small jump seat off to the side. The head of security turned a knob, which caused a door to slide closed between the passenger section and the driver's compartment, partially blocking Lucas from the back. Magnus then removed the two key cards from the silver card reader. He pocketed them and hopped off the bus.

If Lucas was ever going to have a chance at spoiling this Brainwashing Ceremony or finding out about his mother, he would have to beat Ms. Günerro at her own game and use her rules against her. He would have to act now.

Ms. Günerro pulled the lever to close the front doors, and without delay the silver card reader flashed with a series of lights. A hydraulic motor behind Lucas's head churned, and a thick shoulder harness dropped into place. The seat belt was right out of a roller coaster ride. Padded metal arms quickly fell over Lucas's neck and chest and locked him and Gini into their seat. As soon as the latch clicked, a video in front of him began.

Ms. Günerro clicked her seat belt and put the Busball bus into gear. The big black bus slowly drove through a thick white cloud of dry ice. It emerged from the fog and continued down a gravel pathway toward the Eiffel Tower. Out the window Lucas could see Astrid, Travis, and Nalini running way ahead of the two guards. But no Hervé. They sprinted under the Eiffel Tower and through a little park, where Ekki and Goper plopped down on a bench.

In front of Lucas a retro black-and-white illusion circled hypnotically on the screen. He knew he shouldn't watch. With one hand he covered Gini's eyes, and with the other he pounded on the bars over his shoulders. The harness didn't budge. Gini didn't seem to like the tight quarters either, and she started to squirm uncomfortably, which gave Lucas an idea.

It had all started two days earlier with Gini in the shopping cart at the Globe Hotel. Lucas had been gambling since then on this little girl, and there was no sense in stopping now. Gini twisted again, and both her arms and head were outside the shoulder harness. Lucas sucked in his gut and pulled Gini's legs around the seat belt. She was free.

The only way to stop the brainwashing video was with key cards. Lucas had two: Boutros's master key card from the Good Hotel, the one that Gini had reactivated with her thumb, and the Globe Hotel key card. Lucas took the hotel key cards from his back pocket and gave them to Gini. He hoped she would remember how to use them. He set Gini on the rubber-padded floorboard, and she crawled toward the driver's seat. Ms. Günerro was distracted. She was frantically trying to shoo carnival kids from the road and didn't seem to notice a baby crawling next to her compartment.

Gini lifted herself up just enough and slotted her first key card. The card that Gini had reactivated in the Lucky Office immediately zapped all the monitors on the bus, just like it had in Ms. Günerro's office. From the back of the bus kids started to grumble as they broke from their video trance. Then Gini inserted the second card, the Globe Hotel key card, and the metal seat belt harnesses unlocked. Kids started to get out of their seats and move around.

Ms. Günerro didn't seem to notice the commotion brewing on the bus. She was still leaning forward over the steering wheel, fixated on the kids in the road.

"Hey, Lucas," Terry called from the back. "Are you up there?"

Lucas didn't respond because he didn't want Ms. Günerro to see him. He crouched on the floor and looked under the gap in the barrier separating the two sections. Terry was running down the aisle to him, and Lucas signaled for the boy to stop and be quiet. Lucas then crawled over to Gini and picked her up. That's when Ms. Günerro saw him. She slammed on the brake, which knocked everyone standing to the floor. Ms. Günerro then threw the bus into low gear and took off.

Lucas and Gini rolled on the floor, and Lucas quickly scrambled to his jump seat. He looked out the window and saw people scattering everywhere, running away from the speeding bus. Lucas spotted Hervé alone with his cane hobbling down a street, Ekki and Goper trotting after him. There was no sign of the others.

The inside of the Busball bus had become an awful carnival ride. As Ms. Günerro started to drive like a lunatic, the kids on the bus began screaming and falling all over one another. With every turn, balls were rolling up and down the center aisle.

Lucas strapped Gini to the jump seat, and then he sprang over to the driver's compartment. He grabbed hold of Ms. Günerro's seat belt strap and pulled himself up. In one sliding motion, he arched his back and flipped his body around. He tried to jam his foot on the brake, but he couldn't quite reach. When he grabbed hold of the steering wheel, the Busball bus twisted wildly through the grass as Lucas and Ms. Günerro began to fight for control. They drove past the giant slide and underneath the tower itself. Crowds scrambled out of the way as the wayward bus weaved circles around Paris's most famous monument.

During this time Gini had climbed down from her seat and crawled into the driver's compartment. She tugged on Ms. Günerro's dress and pulled herself up. The baby seemed to bother her more than ever this time, and for a second the always-in-control CEO let go of the steering wheel.

Ms. Günerro was furious and she reached out to claw Lucas's face with her fingernails. By instinct Lucas snapped his head back. Her nail just nicked his neck, but the distraction was enough to make Ms. Günerro lose control of the bus, and lose control of herself.

"AAAAARGH!" she screamed at Lucas.

The bus swerved then careened toward one of the legs of the tower. Lucas jerked the steering wheel back his way but he overcompensated. The bus cut back into the park, where they drove straight into a park bench. The wooden bench shattered to bits. Still the bus drove on unguided down the park lawn, clipping a line of light poles. The poles snapped like dry trees, and the big white streetlamps of the Champ de Mars exploded on impact. The Busball bus then smashed through a fence and mowed through the center of a grassy area, knocking over bushes and benches, and eventually blasting onto a busy sidewalk.

Everyone was shouting and scrambling in all directions. Lucas was sure the bus was going to run someone over. Kids on the bus were squealing and howling so loudly that it became hard to think. Lucas's mind was cluttered. He tried again to stomp on the brake. Instead Ms. Günerro stamped his foot onto the gas pedal. Lucas grabbed the back of her seat and held on. With her foot on top of his, they picked up speed until the bus dropped off the curb and smashed into two parked cars, spinning them up and onto the sidewalk. Lucas finally yanked his foot free from the gas pedal, let go of the wheel, and scooped Gini up into his arms.

Ms. Günerro, now back in full control, loomed over the steering wheel like a mad fugitive. It was as if she had planned this whole crazy getaway. Again she gunned it, only to slam on the brake at the next intersection, fishtailing the big bus in the crosswalks. Kids on the bus went crashing into the windows. Lucas slipped and nearly tossed Gini out the front doors.

The bus swerved left and right and headed straight for a group of people who were staring up at the Eiffel Tower. Lucas set Gini on the floor then dove back and slapped the steering wheel to avoid hitting the crowd. Ms. Günerro jerked the wheel her way and cut across a bridge. The big black bus slammed into a railing bordering the river. The old concrete wall gave way as the Busball bus crashed through the barrier and plunged, headlights first, into the river.

A wave of water engulfed the bus, but it popped up and floated, rocking back and forth on the water.

For a second.

Ms. Günerro snarled at Lucas. "If you really were on that ferryboat when it sank," she said with pure evil in her eyes, "then you are probably not too keen on water."

Lucas didn't understand. At all. The Busball bus was amphibious, made for both land and water. The only way it could sink was if . . .

He hadn't even finished the thought when Ms. Günerro reached over and clutched the door lever. "Not as cold as Antarctic waters," Ms. Günerro seethed, "but dark enough to make you tell me where you and your mother hid my accounts." She tugged on the door handle, but it didn't move. She hit some sort of bypass button, and then with two hands she wrenched the front doors open.

Water flooded the bus. It came quickly as the nose of the Busball bus slowly tilted downward. The kids and balls began rumbling down toward the front compartment. Lucas then felt the first wave of water lapping at his shoes. Within seconds, river water hit the electrical system and blue lights flickered across the dashboard.

Lucas reached down to grab Gini but she was gone.

"Gini," he called over the voices of the screaming kids.

Lucas jumped back diagonally and hit a button, which opened the door separating the front and back compartments. He looked up the aisle for Gini. A group of kids were sliding out of control. Still holding onto the Busball balls they had won, three kids slipped straight down the aisle and crashed into Lucas. One of them knocked the door lever, nudging the front doors open even farther. More river water gushed into the ever-growing pool.

Lucas quickly wrapped both of his hands around the lever and closed the two front doors.

As the kids clawed their way back up the bus, the safety lights lining the center aisle died in an orderly but dramatic burst.

Lucas turned and focused on his real problem.

Ms. Günerro had taken weird to a new level. She was sitting in the driver's seat, wiping off the steering wheel with a handkerchief of some kind. Lucas didn't and couldn't understand what she was doing. Or why.

"What are you doing?" Lucas shouted. He grabbed the steering wheel. "This is an amphibious bus. Turn the bus up. We're going to sink if you don't drive. You can still save it."

Ms. Günerro smiled evilly, as if everything were going according to plan.

"This bus is not worth a fraction of the money held in the bank accounts that you have the numbers and codes to."

"I don't know how many times I have to tell you," Lucas screamed, "but I don't have your stupid money or codes!"

"Oh," she said. "But you do."

Lucas was beyond confused. He was standing in a bus in ankle-deep water. Kids at the back of the bus were screaming because the bus was floating in a river. And slowly sinking. Balls of all kinds were floating and bouncing around the bus. He couldn't find Gini. Crowds of people were watching from the banks and from the broken bridge. Jackknife and the others were in Madame Beach's boat, speeding downriver toward the bus. And Ms. Günerro was calmly sitting in her seat with a handkerchief, wiping everything she had touched.

"Are you nuts?" Lucas shouted. "Why are you wiping everything off?"

"Because," said Ms. Günerro almost proudly, "when the underwater forensics are completed on this accident, it will be your fingerprints on the steering wheel and everything else. And you will be blamed for having caused all of this."

With the handkerchief, Ms. Günerro then opened her side window. Slowly but steadily water began to flood the bus.

Drowning in dark water had always been Lucas's greatest fear. But worse than that was the horror of letting so many other kids drown with him. They would all surely die. Maybe he was supposed to have died in the ferry accident when he was a baby. He shook the thoughts away.

The bus tilted downward, and water seeped in from every tiny crack in the bus. A flicker of light pulsed throughout the whole bus, and then a huge flash lit up the river as the headlights flared and then exploded. An explosion on dark water. The whole bus went black and all the kids screamed.

"Everybody," Lucas shouted above the noise. "Go to the back of the bus and climb through the safety hatch in the roof!"

The three other New Resistance members—Sora, Kerala, and Terry—took charge. Kids were crying as they scrambled to the back of the bus. Nearly everyone crammed into an area just outside the toilet. Sora and Kerala climbed up on the last two seats and straddled the aisle with their feet balanced on two headrests. With black makeup running down her cheeks, Kerala popped open the safety hatch in the roof and helped Terry climb out.

"Lucas," Terry yelled into the now dark bus. "Jack-knife and the others are here with a boat. Come on."

The bus then turned sideways and hundreds of balls shifted in the seats and flooded the center walkway. Lucas kicked several basketballs out of his way as he turned his attention back to Ms. Günerro, who was sitting patiently in the driver's seat as if the chaos on the bus were perfectly normal.

Sora and Kerala started pushing kids up through the safety hatch to Terry. Within a minute Jackknife's boat was full. Through the window Lucas could see the hull of Madame Beach's boat as it sped to a platform bordering the river. There the first group got off the boat, and Jackknife spun it back to the sinking bus.

Lucas needed to focus. First he had to find Gini and get her out of the bus. He called her name again and again. But nothing. Then he heard a peep. From the storage compartment above the driver's seat, Gini giggled. And in one motion she jumped like a flying squirrel—right on top of Ms. Günerro's head.

"AAAAARGH!" Ms. Günerro screamed as she swatted Gini out of her hair. Lucas quickly snatched the baby away, and while Ms. Günerro tried to calm down, he fought his way up the rubber-padded aisle with Gini clutched tight to his side.

The next group of would-be brainwashed kids boarded Jackknife's boat and took off. With fewer people now on the bus, the weight shifted and the bus tilted again and pointed almost straight down. Lucas lost his balance and slid down the wet aisle into the balls floating around the dashboard.

After three ferrying trips, everyone was safely on the platform except Lucas, Gini, and Ms. Günerro.

"Lucas," Travis yelled down through the safety hatch. "Come on."

Lucas yelled back, "Throw me a rope."

Travis tossed the boat rope down the center aisle of the bus and into the rising water. Lucas tied a quick bowline and wrapped it around Gini's shoulders. Travis then hoisted Gini up through the middle of the bus and out the safety hatch.

"Come on, Lucas," pleaded Travis. "The boat's here."

If Ms. Günerro had planned all of this, then Lucas would have to play along. He knew if he was ever going to find out about his birth mother and where he'd come from, he would need Ms. Günerro alive. And she would need him for the account numbers that he didn't have.

"I'll be right there," said Lucas with a touch of irony in his voice. "I've got Ms. Günerro's number and I have to give it to her."

Gini was safe and Lucas could do what he needed to. When he turned to Ms. Günerro, Lucas found her still buckled in the driver's seat, but she had exchanged her rhinestone mask for a rhinestone scuba mask and snorkel.

The nose of the bus twisted and angled diagonally as it corkscrewed toward the bottom of the river.

Water was coming from everywhere now. The force of this new water seemed to pin Ms. Günerro back in her seat. She flailed her arm to get to her seat belt lock, but there were too many balls in the way. With the water rising and the seat belt still locked, Ms. Günerro suddenly panicked.

For Lucas it was an opportunity.

Deep down he just wanted to punch her in the face. Instead Lucas ripped her scuba mask off and chucked it into the flooded bus.

Ms. Günerro barked at him, "Give me my glasses! My mask!"

Lucas flung his wet hair to the side. "Not until you give me what I want."

"What do you want?"

"I want my mother."

"I don't have your mother."

"Well then," said Lucas, "you don't get your scuba mask."

Lucas needed information more than anything. But how could he force Ms. Günerro to tell him about his mother? She might not care about her ugly mask, but she certainly would care about her life. Wouldn't she?

River water now covered the entire front of the bus. The metal chassis groaned, and Lucas could feel the bus physically going straight down. The water pressure grew stronger, which pushed him farther from Ms. Günerro and closer to drowning. Ms. Günerro slapped around in the water and found her scuba mask.

Against his greatest fear, Lucas took a huge breath and plunged head down into the cold dark water. He slapped around on the rubber floor, and next to her seat he bumped into the stick shift. Then he found what he was looking for. He briefly popped up for air and dove again. This time he grabbed a metal clip on the side of the seat belt.

The waterline was now at Ms. Günerro's neck.

"Undo my seat belt!" Ms. Günerro commanded as she put her scuba mask back on.

Lucas pulled on the seat belt and the shoulder strap wrenched Ms. Günerro into the seat.

"Gladly," said Lucas. "As soon as you tell me what happened to my mother."

"She died on that ferry," said Ms. Günerro. "Now undo the seat belt! I can't move my arms."

"I don't mean my adoptive mother," said Lucas as he slapped a clump of tennis balls out of the way. "I mean my birth mother."

Lucas jerked her seat belt again. Two basketballs floated together, splashing river water into Ms. Günerro's mouth.

"You're going to kill me?" she asked as if taunting him. "Do you want that on your conscience?"

Lucas's legs started to float in the rising water. He held on tight to the seat belt clip that could save the woman who had killed Astrid's mother and possibly his own. He knew he would feel awful if he swam away and let her drown in the bus. Letting her die just wasn't right.

Lucas paddled the basketballs away from Ms. Günerro's face, but she seemed to have another plan. She put the snorkel in her mouth and let her head sink below the water's surface. Lucas figured it was a trick. He stabbed his hand into the water and ripped the snorkel out of her mouth. Ms. Günerro's head popped above the waterline and she coughed as she took the snorkel back.

Lucas screamed in her face. "What happened to my mother?"

"Give me the account number first," she said, "and I'll give you your mother."

"I don't know how many times I need to tell you," said Lucas, "but I don't know the account numbers you're talking about."

"Kate Benes gave you some numbers and passwords."

"That's not true."

"Your mother gave Kate Benes those numbers and codes," said Ms. Günerro. "I. Know. This."

"Then they are lost forever."

"No, Kate Benes gave them to you," said Ms. Günerro. "What did you have with you when she put you in that ice chest?"

"How did you know about the ice chest?"

"Nuns are weak."

In his mind Lucas flipped through the pages of his birth chart. The doctors said he was an FLK. A Funny

Looking Kid. Was that code for something else? There were numbers everywhere on his chart, and cryptic doctor scribble. Was this what she was talking about?

"All I had with me," said Lucas, "was the bell the nuns gave me. That's all."

Ms. Günerro stretched her neck so she could put the snorkel back in her mouth. She mumbled, "Your mother could have had an accident by now. You just don't know."

"So then my mother, my birth mother, *is* still alive?"

"Of course she is," said Ms. Günerro. She removed the snorkel from her mouth. "I knew you'd come looking for your mommy one day."

"So where is she?"

"You'll undo the seat belt?"

"I promise. And I don't break promises," said Lucas. "As soon as you tell me where my mother is."

More water poured in and little foam footballs floated into Lucas's view.

Lucas was livid. "Where is she?" he said as he yanked on the seat belt strap.

Ms. Günerro choked and coughed and put the snorkel back in her mouth. Then she blew water from the snorkel's spout.

She clenched the snorkel in her teeth. "Argentina," she muttered.

Lucas clicked her seat belt free. "You're on your own now."

Then he swam up through the flooded aisles and to the back of the bus. At the escape hatch he paused and looked back down into the dark water in the bus. He couldn't see Ms. Günerro at all.

GOOD THINGS HAPPEN TO BAD PEOPLE

From a floating dock, Lucas and the others watched the bumper and license plate of the bus sink into the dark river. The bus was obviously only semi-amphibious. Lucas thought it was fitting for a bus made by the Good Company—pretty on the outside and rotten on the inside.

At the same time two police boats raced to the scene from upriver. Divers plunged into the river and stayed underwater for what seemed like a very long time. Lucas thought that maybe he had been too slow and that Ms. Günerro had drowned. He didn't want to kill anyone, not even Siba Günerro. He wondered if not helping her get out was a crime.

A few seconds later another boat similar to the police boats buzzed to the opposite bank. The boat stopped, and the officers on that boat shone giant beams of light down into the water. After a few passes of the light, Ms. Günerro's head rose above the surface. She lifted the scuba mask, and one of the officers removed a small air tank from her back. The officers then pulled Ms. Günerro into the police boat. Lucas and the others then saw the peach-fuzz mustaches on the police officers. The boy at the hostel had been right. The Good Company had many pirate boats in Paris—they just looked like police boats.

While the real police officers circled the sunken bus, Ms. Günerro and her personal police boys sped away and into the night.

A HOTEL IS A HOME

Coach Creed, Robbie, and Sophia gathered everyone into a waiting van, which took them to a private landing strip outside Paris. The inside of the plane looked terrible. The frames of the electronic doors were burned, and the monitors were blank. No one seemed to care. The kids all crashed in their respective seat pods. They were all there: Lucas, Astrid, Jackknife, Nalini, Travis, Terry, Kerala, Sora. All of them. With the sleeping baby on his shoulder, Lucas reclined. He thought about Hervé for a second. He hoped they would see him again.

Lucas felt the plane taxiing down the runway, and the moment they took off, he fell dead asleep.

Sometime thereafter the enormous doors to the New Resistance airplane hangar reopened. The line of kids trudged from the plane to the train to the moving sidewalks and finally to the elevator.

As he dragged his noodle legs down the hall to his room, Lucas felt like he was walking in a hallway filled with ketchup. He didn't brush his teeth and didn't even notice that the window, the curtain, and the air-conditioning vent had all been fixed.

Housekeeping had put a crib in the room, and Lucas set Gini on the mattress with a little plush doll. He didn't even think about sleeping on the roof. He collapsed into bed and pulled the covers to his shoulders.

For fourteen years Lucas Benes believed his mother, his birth mother, to be dead. But with the Good Company, things were not always as they seemed. That night Lucas Benes lay in a bed in his hotel room, dreaming about a past he knew he *could* remember. He dreamed what it would be like once he found his mother, his birth mother, alive.

A CALL TO ACTION

**Do the write thing.
Write a review online!**

⭐⭐⭐⭐⭐

www.bit.ly/crimetravelers

Get Crime Travelers Book 2:
Diamonds Are For Never

After sabotaging a mass kidnapping in Paris, Lucas Benes faces a new and perilous threat from Siba Günerro and her anything-but-good Good Company.

When a briefcase-toting kid from the Falkland Islands joins the New Resistance, 14-year-old Lucas learns the truth about his mother and becomes a boy on a mission.

Lucas and friends speed in and around Rome—from the Colosseum to the Vatican—until they stowaway on a cargo ship carrying diamonds that could unlock the secret to Lucas's past and destroy the Good Company's future.

Visit www.crimetravelers.com
for information on speech & Skype requests.